HOR

By

Peter Preston

Hor

ISBN: 978-1-326-46873-6

Third Print Edition: Bloomsbury-Alpha Press
London.
verticaline@hotmail.com

First published in 1997 by Online Originals,
London and Bordeaux.

Hor is dedicated to the memory of my mother.

The Barque of Re which carries the gods Hu and Sia together with The Steersman, The Maiden of the Hour and the serpent, Mehen. Flesh-of-Re stands beneath the naos-canopy.

Introduction

The civilisation of Ancient Egypt lasted for over three thousand years. During this time the Egyptian religious beliefs remained largely unchanged with the notable exception of the period of *Aten*-worship during the eighteenth dynasty under Akhenaten. Even more remarkable, the mythology, for the most part, reveals itself as already fully-formed when the first hieroglyphic writing in which it is recorded emerged in the period prior to the first dynasty.

This pantheon consisted principally in animal-gods represented in the iconography as animal-headed men and women in which the head represented the identity of the deity while the divine attributes became incorporated into the body. Thus there were the familiar hawk-headed *Horus* and jackal-headed *Anubis,* the ibis-headed *Thoth* and the others. Notable exceptions, however, were the important deities, *Re* and *Osiris*, who emerged at the time of the third and fifth dynasties respectively.

Re was the sun-god and underwent several transformations during the course of his daily passage through the sky and through the Underworld at night. He became *Atum* at sunset, *Flesh-of-Re* during the night and *Khepri* at dawn before returning to his day form, *Re.*

Osiris was a deity of fully human appearance who suffered a death and was credited with a form of resurrection which in many ways prefigures that of Christ. Certainly in his resurrected form, *Osiris* became the judge and ruler of the dead.

Creation myths abounded in the Egyptian mythology. Remarkably, the apparent contradictions between these various beliefs were likely to trouble the Egyptian mind much less than they do that of modern man. For example, the deities *Re, Atum, Ptah, Neith* and a mysterious group of eight primordial beings known as the *Ogdoad* were variously believed to have been responsible for the Creation itself or at least the origin of man. However, these conflicting views were not seen to be contradictory by the Egyptian tradition which was one of compromise and reconciliation. Thus these rival claims were either assimilated one with another or else allowed to stand beside each other as alternative truths. They therefore served as different aspects of a central mystery.

Similarly, the identity of the supreme god varied from place to place and from time to time. *Re, Atum, Amun, Ptah* have all at times been considered paramount in this way. Indeed, the cult of *Osiris* was so firmly based that the sacred texts describing the night journey of the sun-god, *Re*, through the Underworld place *Osiris* rather than *Re* as king of that Underworld. *Re,* in fact, passes from sunset to sunrise through the kingdom of the resurrected *Osiris.*

The three main sacred texts describing this journey are to be found inscribed on the interior walls within rock-cut tombs of the pharaohs of the New Kingdom such as that of *Rameses VI.* They are the *Book of Gates,* the *Book of Am Duat* and the *Book of Caverns.* Other texts exist such as the *Book of Night and Day* and there are many individual spells to be found on papyri from burials of nobles and commoners alike. These spells are collectively known as *The Book of the Dead*. It is from these sources, principally, that the material for this present book derives.

The Ancient Egyptians believed that after death the self survived as a complex of three spirit forms. With life gone from the *khat* or body, the *ba* or 'soul of movement' and the *ka* or 'soul of sustenance' manifested themselves. The third spirit form, the *akh*, was thought of as the totality of the transfigured self and possessed the divine power to transform itself into different modes of existence.

The *ba,* demonstrating both the identity of the individual and the attribute of *mobility*, took the form of a human head on the body of a bird while the *ka* was considered the double of the person concerned. It was through this spirit form that sustenance for the whole complex was maintained.

From texts such as the *Book of Night and Day* alternative descriptions of the passage of the sun from dusk to dawn arise - in this case along and through the naked body of the sky goddess, *Nut,* conceived as arching overhead and forming the firmament.

As well as the three descriptions of the Underworld in the three main sacred texts there was also a multiplicity of paradises for the Ancient Egyptian. Roughly comparable to the *Elysean Fields* was a watery paradise: *The Field of Reeds.* The horizon was also thought of as the destination of righteous souls after death. But an echo of a still earlier belief system placed a heaven among the circumpolar stars which circle the celestial north pole in such a way as never to rise or set.

The priests of the different cult centres in Egypt were able to reconcile these conflicting theologies, creation myths, paradises and visions of hell. In fact, it is in no small measure due to their relative success in this endeavour that the religion of these ancients remained as the stable heart of such a long-lived and cohesive civilisation.

These patterns of belief of the Ancient Egyptians were formerly only accessible to later scholars through Greek and Roman writers contemporary with the later dynasties. As such these were second-hand accounts. This was because the various scripts used by the Egyptians were not translated until after the discovery of the Rosetta stone by Napoleonic troops. This remarkable tablet bears parallel Greek and hieroglyphic texts and thus formed the basis for the decipherment of the Egyptian written language.

These then are the myths and ancient religious beliefs which have formed the basis for the present book - a work of the imagination composed in the twentieth century.

Reaching back to these past currents of thought has required the assistance of modern-day scholarship and the present writer wishes to acknowledge the invaluable assistance of Professor Stephen Quirke formerly of the Department of Egyptian Antiquities at the British Museum who has spent time both advising on the Egyptian mythology and later checking the manuscript for mythological accuracy while under a heavy work load of his own.

Peter Preston
London, 2015

Glossary

(Entries in the sequence required by the main text.)

Montu: Hawk-headed war god of Thebes.

Horus: Son of Isis and Osiris. Hawk-headed god identified with the *ka* of the pharaoh. Avenged the death of Osiris by prolonged battle with Seth.

Thoth: Ibis-headed god of wisdom and writing. Assists at judgement of the dead.

Atum: Form of the sun-god at sunset. Atum takes the form of an old man leaning on a stick.

Apis Bull: Sacred bull of Ptah.

Re: Sun-god. Creator god according to most prominent myth. Undergoes daily journey through the skies and into the Underworld during which Re is successively transformed into the following deities: Atum, Flesh-of-Re, Khepri and again Re. Chief deity of The Ennead. Father of Shu and Tefnut.

Pharaoh: Title of Egyptian kings in use from the New Kingdom onwards. However, the term has come to be used to describe Egyptian rulers from all dynasties. For clarity, the present text uses the term in this widest sense.

Unas: Fifth dynasty pharaoh possessing a prominent pyramid tomb in which wall texts describe him eating the gods.

Saïs: City of the Delta on Rosetta branch of the Nile. Modern-day Sa El-Hagar.

Duat: Ancient Egyptian Underworld. Three different descriptions of the Underworld are provided by the three sacred texts: *The Book of Caverns, The Book of Am Duat* and *The Book of Gates.*

Maidens of the Hours: Goddesses of the Underworld responsible for each hour of the journey of Flesh-of-Re.

Rosetjau: Mythical site of entry into the Underworld. Originally the name of the royal necropolis at Giza.

Night Barque: The sacred boat upon which Flesh-of-Re travels through the Underworld. Also known as Barque of Re, Solar Barque etc. The daytime journey takes place in the Day Barque.

Opening of the Mouth: Funerary ceremony performed on inanimate objects such as coffins, statues or the dead themselves and designed to 'open the mouth' and enable them to receive sustenance for life.

khat: Body of individual after death.

ka: The double or 'soul of sustenance' - one of three souls of Ancient Egyptian belief.

ba: The Ancient Egyptian 'soul of mobility'. In funerary texts the *ba* is shown in the form of a human-headed bird.

akh: Third soul of the Ancient Egyptians - the illuminating principle.

sem-**priest**: Officiant at funerary rites depicted wearing a panther-skin robe.

shabti-**figures**: Figurines buried with the mummy which are meant to accompany the departed after death and do work for the soul.

Field of Reeds: One of several paradises of Ancient Egypt. An earthly paradise like the Elysian Fields.

Anubis: Jackal-headed god of mummification.

djed-**column**: Cult symbol of stability. The appearance is of a tree trunk with four short-cut horizontal branches on either side. The *djed*-column is said to represent the backbone of Osiris.

Osiris: Prominent deity within the Ennead. Son of Geb and Nut. Brother and husband of Isis and father of their son, Horus. Osiris was god of vegetation and rebirth but was murdered by Seth. Importantly he was god of the Underworld and judge of the dead.

Isis: Wife and sister of Osiris and sister of Nephthys and Seth. Conceived Horus from the dead body of Osiris while she was in the form of a kite-bird. Revived Osiris and protected Horus as a child until he was old enough to do battle with Seth and avenge his father Osiris.

Seth: Red, war-like and wrathful god. Murderer of his brother, Osiris. Husband of his own sister, Nephthys. Fought Horus and was eventually forced to give up the kingship. Said to have torn himself from his own mother's womb at birth.

Two lands: The kingdom of the two lands is a way of describing Upper and Lower Egypt after their unification.

was-**sceptre**: Pharaonic symbol of kingship.

Festival of the lamps: Night festival which took place in Saïs where lamps were placed about the citizens' dwellings.

Nun: Chaotic primeval waters from which the creator god emerged. See also: Amun and Amaunet, Eightfold writhing differences.

Neith: Female creator god according to one myth. Neith gave birth to herself. She also gave birth to Apopis sometimes known as *The Spittle of Neith.*

Ennead: The name of the group of nine principal gods according to the most prominent creation myth. First generation: Re (Atum); second generation: Shu and Tefnut; third generation: Geb and Nut; fourth generation: Osiris, Seth, Isis, Nephthys.

Shu: God of air and light. See Tefnut.

Khnemu: Ram-headed god associated with the Nile cataracts. Controller of the annual inundation.

Tefnut: Goddess of mist. Shu and Tefnut were created in the Nun by their father Atum or Re.

Geb: God of the earth. Son of Shu and Tefnut. Consort of Nut.

Nut: Goddess of the sky, particularly the night sky. She is very beautiful and the stars appear along her naked body. She is said to swallow the sun at sunset and give birth to it at dawn. Mother of Osiris, Isis, Seth and Nephthys.

Bennu bird: A phoenix-like bird. The Bennu was the *ba* of Re.

Atef crown: Crown particular to Osiris and characteristically flanked by twin plumes.

Nephthys: Sister of Isis, wife of brother Seth, one-time lover of brother Osiris. Assisted Isis in evading the wrath of Seth after his murder of Osiris.

Emmer: Ancient Egyptian species of wheat.

Sia: God of Perception personified.

Hu: God of the Word personified.

Ptah: Creator god according to a myth centred upon Memphis. God of crafts.

Barque of Re: see Night Barque.

Underworld: See Duat.

Khepri: Form of the sun-god at dawn. Khepri takes the form of a scarab beetle. At times referred to as *'The Becoming'*. See Scarab.

Sekhmet: Lion-headed goddess.

Nefertum: God of perfume.

Assessor Gods: The forty-two gods who attend at the weighing of the heart ceremony and who assess the soul of a dead person as he professes his innocence.

Judgement of the dead: Ceremony taking place in the sixth hour of the Duat in which the heart is weighed against the feather of Maat (truth). The Assessor Gods hear the profession of innocence and Osiris presides overall.

Tatenen: God symbolising the emergence of the fertile Nile silt after the inundation.

Seker: Hawk-headed god of the Underworld. More accurately god of another underworld within the Underworld. Seker is thought of as the personification of the despairing cry of Osiris.

Udjat: Eye of Horus restored after being injured by Seth. The udjat eye is therefore a symbol of perfection.

Min: God of fertility and of rainstorms.

Decans: Thirty-six star groups from which the passage of time was measured.

Unwearying Stars: Stars which rise and set as normal. Such stars are thought to accompany Flesh-of-Re in the Underworld. Among these stars are the decans.

Imperishable Stars: The circumpolar stars of the northern sky. Such stars are so close to the pole that they do not rise or set (cf. *'The Plough'* or *'Big Dipper'* in contemporary skies). They represent a paradise available to the pharaohs and the gods.

Punt: Fabled southern land probably near to present-day Somalia.

Bakhu: Mythical mountain of the sunrise.

Ptah-Tatenen: Assimilated form of the gods Ptah and Tatenen.

Mound: Feature of one of the Egyptian creation myths. The earth emerges from the Nun as a mound - just as islands are seen to appear in the Nile following the inundation.

Sons of Horus: Hapy, Imsety, Duamutef, Qebehsenuef. Four gods who appear widely throughout the mythology. Their heads appear on canopic jars of human viscera at mummification. They also represent the cardinal points, north, south, east and west. Their tresses were said to keep up the four corners of heaven. They appear with Osiris at the judgement of the dead.

Ureaus: Cobra with erect hood showing arousal.

Amemet: Devouring monster of the Underworld. Amemet eats the souls of the guilty.

Maat: Goddess of order, truth and rightfulness.

Solar Barque: See Night Barque, Barque of Re.

Meretseger: Serpent goddess worshipped near the Valley of the Kings in western Thebes.

Gubla: Ancient Mediterranean seaport situated at what is now Jubayl in Lebanon.

Apopis: The Ancient Egyptian personification of evil. Apopis is a huge serpent in the Underworld who attacks Flesh-of-Re but is defeated by him. Apopis is first encountered in the waters of Nun where he represents darkness and chaos. According to another myth Apopis is the offspring of Neith and is known as the *'Spittle of Neith'*.

Hapi: God of the Nile.

The Becoming: See Khepri.

Atum-Re: Assimilated form of the two gods Atum and Re.

Aker: Lion-headed god of the Underworld. Represented as twin-headed: facing both the sunset and the dawn.

Sobek: Crocodile god.

naos-**canopy**: Canopy on the Barque of Re protecting Flesh-of-Re. The canopy is protected by the body of the serpent, Mehen.

Coming forth into day: The idea of the earthly wandering of the *ka*-soul after death.

Scarab: Egyptian dung-beetle. Symbol of rebirth of the sun and therefore of Khepri, the form of the sun-god at dawn.

River of Urnes: River of the Underworld.

Flesh-of-Re: Form of the sun-god in his travels through the Underworld. Dead form of Re depicted as a standing, ram-headed man.

The Steersman: The pilot of the Barque of Re.

Mehen: serpent covering the naos-canopy of the Barque of Re.

ba-**souls of Pe**, *ba*-**souls of Nekhen**: Souls of primordial, pre-dynastic kings of Upper and Lower Egypt said to act as protectors of the incumbent pharaoh.

Mut: Theban mother goddess. Consort of Amun.

The Opener of the Ways: See Wepwawet.

The Lady of the Barque: The Maiden of the Hour specific to each particular cave or hour.

Dance of the Muu: Ritual dance performed at the tombside which conjures up the presence of the ba-souls of Pe.

Eightfold writhing differences: Alternative creation myth. Eight deities both male and female having snake- and frog-heads represent the primordial darkness, invisibility, inertness and nothingness. Known as the *Ogdoad*.

Amun, Amaunet: With Nun and Naunet, Heh and Hauket, Kek and Kauket - the gods and their corresponding goddesses forming the Ogdoad.

Nomarch: Governor of an Egyptian province.

Wenen-Nofer: A form of Osiris.

Eye of Re: The motif of the Eye in Ancient Egyptian art. The Eye of Re is said to have an independent existence.

Wepwawet: Jackal-headed god associated with Anubis and known as the *Opener Of The Ways*.

Barge of the Earth: A feature of the Underworld perhaps representing an earlier concept of a Duat. The Barque of Re is pulled through a bull's mouth and through the spine. An underworld within the Underworld.

Hennu boat: Boat motif associated with Seker.

Khonsu: Moon-god of Thebes associated with Unas. Child of the primeval god, Amun and of his consort, Mut. Sometimes depicted as hawk-headed.

Serquet: Scorpion goddess who attacks Apopis.

Hentiu: Snake-headed gods who attack Apopis.

Spittle of Neith: see Neith, Apopis.

Herakhiti: The form of Horus seen on the horizon.

Harmachis: Horus of the Great Sphinx at Giza.

Horus of Behdet: Horus in the form of a winged disc.

Sothis: The star, Sirius, assimilated to the goddess, Isis.

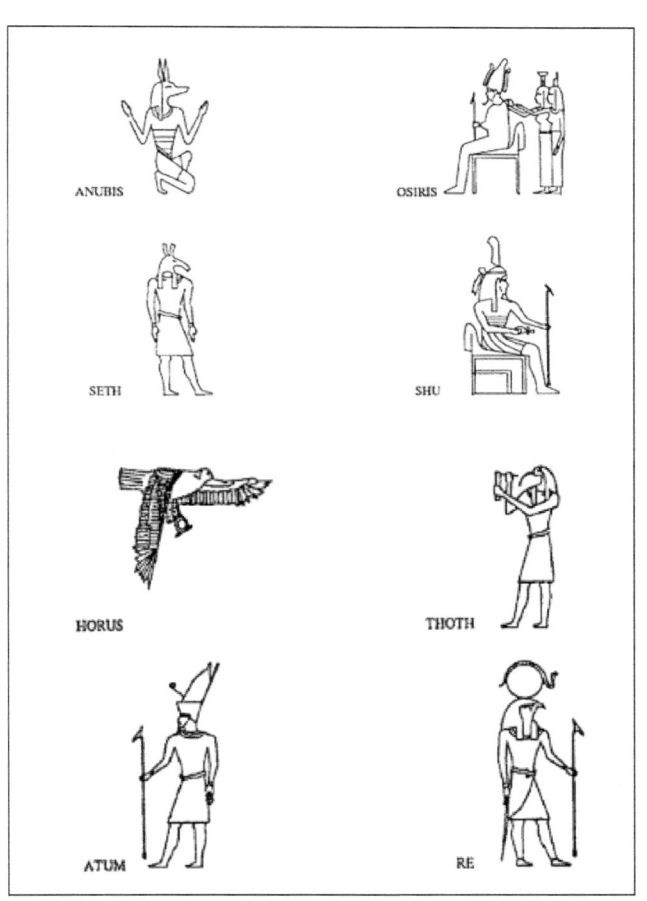

MIN

KHEPRI: THE SCARAB
THE BECOMING

NAOS-CANOPY
AND MEHEN

FLESH-OF-RE

TEFNUT

GEB AND NUT

NEFERTUM

SEKER

Chapter One

HOR

The mummy, the pharaoh Unas and the city of Saïs, spirit forms and the Underworld, Seth and the death of Osiris.

Hor, gatherer of oils, priest of Montu, opener of the gates of heaven in Luxor, son of Ankhori and son of Karem; Hor, at one with Horus and Thoth, enshrined with Atum and carried to the cemetery with the Apis Bull; Hor stood silent in the dark corner.

And the light came from the moonbeams on ox-yokes and scarabs, on the remains of eels, crocodiles, the fish dead from the Nile; on jars of viscera from the city of Saïs - the light on the cartonnage where the occasional visitor might stand. And there were moonbeams that once moved with the rise of the Nile - in green - with weeds flowing in the smallest mud river mouths where birds and insects circled for succour and moved in the mud-filled way; where sands abraded stone faces and other features - the largest features of pediments at Waset - where these grains settled taking with them small impressions to be later distilled, made the essence of every recorded word - in reed-bed river mouths and culled by tired hands, by arms burned with the finer speckles of water heated by bright rays of the sun nearly straight overhead - the ancient sun of changed green plants moving and always decaying into upright remnants. And the moonlight had made unaccustomed movement through the wrong passages built for the sun: discordant, moving over the smoothed inner structure of temples of stone; warmed and cracked by rays failing in their way too but exciting the other features not dreamt of and only apparent at certain times and in places whose sanctity might be disturbed; caught at some further moment and transformed into the slight tremor of other movements of figures and faces perhaps never seen.

In the corridor the moonbeams passed through cabinets - to the first five-stringed harp, of wood from the hottest forests eaten by termites, eaten by the slow passage of water down twisted stems moving in the slight breeze from openings overhead; fashioned in great heat - by bending under water, under sun and the compression of great weights; painted by captive hands occasionally supplicating, submitting certainly, and motioning their efforts and all forms of appeasement, the grief of distorted lives and the reflection instead of sunlight on smooth surfaces.

The harp might then sound.

The sounding chord would spread through temples and to fields and over waterways and into small copses in bright sunlight to where sands might reach further still - with wave motions - with the gentle lift of palm leaves. The chord: more easily heard - by attendant figures dressed in white, moving towards stone structures carrying lamps, precious metal, the tokens of belief.

Hor, bringer of light. Hor enclosed, wrapped and dried, bound in the form of a final agony. Penetrated, scoured, reamed and bruised, broken. Hor, made permanent and the sentinel of nights and days: Hor, guardian, calculator, collector; the singer of melodies beyond understanding, beyond belief and hope.

The rising hope which all accept but only becomes true each moment, Hor - illuminated, preserved, made the image of deep, violent, heated movement beneath the earth; Hor, drawn to movements of sun, stars, the moon - Hor, the preserver.

The largest image in a landscape of forms, rising vertically towards the sun. In each corner the greatest ideas conceived hopefully: the expression of pain; the motions of stars described - and the way, too, light reflects singly from bubbles and droplets. Perpetual, penetrating rich wood and stone buildings. The city.

Compounded, heaped upon, bound up - the repository of all papyri, tallied records, offerings, notes of inventory; the calculation of mass, grain and water reserves, of labour and the engagement of the greatest forces; of adventures and battles; the flow of the Nile over many summers.

There is anxiety about the cost of jade, ivory, camphor, salt; there are the arrivals of plagues and movements of great bodies of water which flow over all lands unequally, which move between islands and wear at rocks and small steps set into temples - and at toll houses, statues to Horus; the sun-god, Re; the great pharaoh, Unas - Unas, himself.

And there is the victim of these nights in palaces, moving between pillars, draperies: in the dark, only the glint of precious metal visible - and listening all the while. Listening to hushed voices and to the sounding of the harp, voices moving through all tones solicitously, too faint to be heard, too high to be listened to and changing all perceptions with fear and the awareness of whispers.

But whispers were louder than words and filled the available space. With these sounds lesser kings might tremble and the high of the land break with accustomed ritual, give way to tremors which might spread through the valley, move over mud flatlands, disturb village life and echo in wells and fields.

Through courtyards first and from one chamber to the next, what Unas touched resounded: guards lowering their heads, weapons falling from their hands.

And dark night birds would take flight.

The moon shifted. Light in the corridor caught the corner where in a busy passageway an occasional visitor might stand, pause, draw out the moment till it became the dry ages of wind-blown sand, the periods when even the path of the sun might change. The visitor knowing all these things would have no need to depart but would float silently on, would pass cabinets and amphorae, move in silence into the air.

But the air would resound and all the hopes and pain of a thousand lives might be assembled and each be made visible to the visitor over fields and ice-sheets. Such visions breaking all accustomed bounds would record dreams of empires. Princes would be brought to account. All that Hor once knew could then become evident and the image of a man would be brought forcefully together. It would be forged as the dreams of Hor had been formed, with moments in summer.

Yet other forms surrounded Hor, circled at every possible moment and gestured where brighter paths might move to left and right and suggest all types of action. These forms might call out as if to be heard and form weak links among themselves. Such vortices cutting themselves off would circle ever more slowly and enter other states completely.

Not every moment lived by Hor would remain accessible, however, and the struggle to reach all would consume time completely. In this way, Hor's life could be entered and the whole would become an effort pursued through centuries. What marked him out could only be such efforts entered gladly, pursued exhaustively and which acted as an aid to others of his kind.

Hor, beset by scarcities; dissembler - Hor, who might survive attacks from small burrowing animals, Hor - *alive!*

Flee! From the disturbance of birth and death; of lives spent comfortably and made the essence of beauty. Of lives regulated - children growing happily, and rewards expected confidently.

Hor's vision was constricted over great distances. There were memories of the efforts of inhabiters of bright crystal - there were fragments of light refracted and broken up, culled from all places equally, understood partially and only assembled in tears by great striving through long years.

There was the sight, through grass of stones on a river bed: distanced, interrupted and made the subject of anger and remorse. The delicate emotion of a child in agony, the recitation of virtues unrecognised, of pain endured silently and never the subject of concern.

Such hope which might surface only gradually and be recognised partially, inhabited the rarest corners in bright days: dark regions such as the spaces between leaves which attract parasitic life. Imagining these would cause tremors and small movements in the available light.

Light which passes through crystals and is favoured by these figures - massed guardians of dreams, the shining custodians dressed in white, translucent, given to the encouragement of every form. Descending, swooping in flight with circles of winds and leaves of summer.

Such figures approach every point and drop scented flowers and aid their rise through uprushing air.

Flowers might carry Hor towards ice and realms undreamed of, these would be delicate moments preserved in centuries.

They rise higher. They rise in Saïs, the city which is where bright lights flicker, arising out of nothing; growing, moving. Such sparkles are reflected and changed - in tunnels, in dwellings, in narrow streets where offerings are made, whispers heard; and the threat spreads outward as the sounding harp is moved.

Oh, city of imagining, glittering in bright sunlight! The people move in wide thoroughfares - always with the awareness of whispers - and there are faces shimmering on open water, there are movements of leaves reflected from surfaces of metal: the closed and intricate paths of collected light, moving between remote regions in distant buildings of the city - merging, refracting, and carrying images composed of every variation possible in the city of light.

The people in this labyrinth, meeting and giving favours, rising and toiling, would feel a single distinct aim. And many had tried to record this hope and had never met with success, had fallen short at the most important moment when all such desires had become fused and perfected.

The representative in full sunlight, to become hopeful, would be swept up, carried through streets with sounding horns, harps, tympani; be welcomed, ushered and celebrated with processions of warriors, adherents, girls, beasts and harvests of fruit and grain.

Initiates would wail, speak in low whispers and resolve secrecy among themselves.

For each of many lives there would be baskets of fruit, corn, gold and emeralds - and essences and oils which Hor had gathered from villages in the delta, from the changing merchants and the grain-lenders, from vessels tied to jetties and plying across hot seas and vessels meeting dangerous currents and the attacks of strangers.

Each boat, brought up short by the grapples of long cables, would be threatened by heavy rams and then would float silently as unknown figures boarded, broke casks and chests open, moved urns and incense jars; stabbed, slashed and conquered every traveller, took every prize.

And the oils would be from Nubia, Punt and Libya and would have been carried through deserts. At other times traders would be found dying beneath desert rocks, and by houses with burdens and beasts standing nearby.

There would be some to offer victims water and there would be others who would be forever unable to make such a gesture. And the soldiers who could prevent these things would turn their faces from such anguish, might never report any sudden deaths and could readily take their prizes wherever they might be found - and thus they gave no accounting, left nothing to chance and in this way continued to prosper.

Hor, in the corridor, erect and your recollections and your desires separated.

The final priestly problem. Of truth, of the fearful outcome to follow death and the records in the tombs of the pharaohs to be reconciled. Oh beauty, and the names of the guardians of the Duat, the Underworld: doorkeepers; the Maidens of the Hours; gods and the enemies of the gods must be spoken. In each text the guides, the last gift of the pharaoh - and in the Book of Caverns, of Gates, of The Two Ways, of Night and Day, of the Am Duat itself are truths for the pharaohs, truths for each vision. The completed images must then merge and the faceted justice, the verities, will be apparent on each examination:

Oh, we know the journey of Re in the night - it is the Book of Gates.

Oh, we know the journey of Re in the Underworld - it is the journey of the Book of Am Duat.

Oh, we know the journey of the Book of Caverns and of the texts in the pyramids, in the coffins, on the wrappings of the dead.

These journeys in one, and at each cavern a single part of the revelation. Descending down passages at Rosetjau, gate of the Underworld, it is possible to see each juncture described in these books. The vision is of journeys which interchange. A myriad alternatives existing. Priestly truths united which differ every time.

The journey each night described; and the tales of the travels fragment and recombine. In the mind the truthful fragments glisten. These gifts, the journeys for the pharaoh: every combination of the night-time passages. The journeys which bifurcate, which spread outward: these are combinations and possibilities each for Hor to lay bare.

For the pharaoh, all routes, passages, paths to be present: the gift, the gift of all truths to be made plain. The path of the solar barque from every different view. All truths thus exist and the alternatives spread outward, forward and into the shadows.

And the journey of Hor may form in the dark, in the night of the ceremony of the Opening of the Mouth.

Hor, the body: the *khat*. Hor, the spirit too: the *ka,* the *ba* and the *akh* - the three forms.

Hor, preserved and wrapped, gilded - the khat of thousands of years - eyes fixed, the amulets and scarabs protecting hope, while all about there is the movement of the double in life - the ka - the spirit subject to gifts and offerings and the tomb-dweller in a land of the night. The ka calls, calls towards the fluttering sound of the bird rising - the ba - spirit of Hor ascending in the air: the movement of vortices in the upper air.

These spirit-forms and hope: souls of man, souls of the son of Ankhori and son of Karem.

To the akh, transforming principle: light, element of spirit and that which shines, shines; which reaches the sun. The akh of Hor, spirit-form, will take up each appearance required. The eternal soul of Hor, unshaped, pure spirit, the changing form.

———————

The calf which bleats cries out in pain and the knife cuts deep. The forelimb separates, is torn from its side, is carried by the white-robed priests towards the table of offerings and the implements for the Opening of the Mouth.

Oh, Hor, your khat in its windings, the newly-dead, the grieved for, the loved form preserved, the priest himself prepared. The perfumed wax upon the head, the lotus before the face - and the light slants gently over the tomb chapel. The pyramid-roof of the tomb chapel and the stele in front of it - upright and casting a long shadow.

From afar the sem-priest approaches clad in the panther's skin and censes the offering table. Oh, the needs of the great journey; the fish and bread loaves, the wine jars and the sickles, hoes, spades and adzes and the shabti-figures who will labour in paradise: oh, will Hor live eternally in the Field of Reeds?

The most precious forms in a land of great wonders: ice and the shining grey glint of the rarest metal. Not the gold, bronze, silver or copper - of each amulet and knife blade; the hard glint of the most precious of implements -

instead the *iron*, iron of the adze to open the way itself. Iron to be pressed to the mouth, the mouth to be opened: Hor's sustenance preserved.

In the form of Anubis, the jackal-headed, the priest known to Hor raises the khat of Hor - Hor in whitened bindings, rigid as the djed-column itself.

And this column of Osiris: firm, the backbone - *stability* - the djed-column to represent the god himself. The column made vertical - and Hor is raised upright too. The adze is brought near to the mouth and the ka of Hor and all spirit-forms of Hor then may be supported - vortices spinning onwards - the ka in the burial chamber and the offering chapel, the ka, simulacrum of Hor in life: the presence, arms raised and calling, calling.

And the ba which might fly across the sky to the god of the setting sun - to Atum; and the akh - light transforming and changed. Oh, akh of Hor: principle of all light, metamorphosis, the desired form reflected, the nature transformed, each feature the expression of the true wish!

Hor in the infinities, Hor joyful and fearful, the rightness of each gesture, the three-fold form; Hor, mouth-opened; and Osiris, Osiris ruler of a night kingdom, able to sustain all agonies peacefully - celebrated at the lake at Saïs, and in such pain - released, drawn up, Osiris would cause Hor's elevation too: thus the long night to come from which Osiris might rise and the corn too; and the old man in the fields and the grateful nation and Khepri's ascension as the morning sun.

But in the Nile, in the casket, Osiris was to die. Buoyed up by warm water lapping, the breath becoming hard: Osiris constrained.

The god screams.

Hands moving frantically, where no chink or fissure runs, hands reaching forward where he might stretch out: Osiris in the coffin, never more to embrace bright day!

Isis, incestuous wife, grieving at Seth's deed and forced into the air would then become the kite-bird which circles above river mouths and searches against the wind with downstroke wingstrokes - hard - above a night river where the sun sets, above the reddened river and the stars of the city and the coiling, heated air. Beneath, birds in level flight, in dark feathers. The city would then become distant, reflected, disturbed.

The air between wings, twisting in vortices brings the dust from a thousand pairs of feet marching - and the sand from faraway winds where no word is ever heard and where the land grows in ridges and tumbles toward red-brown plains. The moving and flickering lights from the horizon illuminate fields and houses, the movements of animals. And in corners of fields and storehouses, by boundary stones where corn accumulates, Isis searches for her lord.

The land from which marvelled forms rise, the study of all forms of reeds and desert flowering plants. Culled in the day, the night, the evening when warm air rises through fronds and through thrusts of insect wings.

The mornings and mist rises over sand and the water's pebbles.

30

Chapter Two

UNAS

The appetites of Unas and the death in the Nile.

The ka of Hor moves: dry days without water, food, air to breathe. Low-hanging limbs of trees with branches dispersed only horizontally - plates, planes of wood and dying green leaves. Birds and insects move and collect at the boles of trees. Centres of decay.

Clouds of spores rise from wounds.

Whispers pass on through ranks and become adapted, reflect the essence of justice, the wisdom of ages. Each refinement grows from the living and the dead. Wisdom rising above simple judgment is loved by the god. Every skill accumulated from dreams and nightmares in Nubia, Punt and Syria is adopted, allocated and used.

Ages of snow. Snow drifting from valleys enters between spurs into spaces underground. Snow gives way at each fissure. Ice is twisted and transformed into liquid between spicules. Every pattern able to reflect the movements in the upper air.

Could any form reflect these changes and twist, rise, revolve, sink, shatter and divide? What figures accumulating in areas of cold could reflect every variation and arise when only slight excess might exist to aid their formation? And every circumstance of their change, the slow ebb of heat - drawn out, sucked, made to filter through grainy matter and particles in suspension, made to pass through each fibre and morsel of organic waste, through the ashes from fires and through desert sands - every feature which might cool becomes covered with broken surfaces, with planes which abut and intersect.

Planes which slip past each other and break in tension and give rise to free-flowing liquid surfaces - each then glinting and refracting - every circumstance then, every response to winds, to variable pressure and to the sun, to the seep of heat into empty space - each moment, every encoded memory and measure of vibration would then cause its own unique form, its delicate increase. Such jewels of the moment, the encoded reflections of mists arising on mountain tops might aggregate and touch solid surfaces - might sparkle, send out brittle fibres, touch and set hard.

Unas, pharaoh, greatest lord looks lustily at each conquered hero; at the cunning of generals. Unas trembles. Unas dreams. A private delight and the pharaoh has learnt the secrets of strength, will, the pleasure of courage; of anger, the governance of the kingdom of the two lands of Egypt - of the Nile. Unas, able to defeat each enemy takes upon himself every strength for the pharaoh has looked enviously at the strongest of men and his eyes have then risen to the heavens. Unas envied the gods.

Unas dreams:

The pharaoh's helpers range wide. Unas might rise and never might take flesh to be eaten nor to be torn from bones. Skulls, then, might never be cracked open in this way, soft meat might never be devoured speedily; blood might never be drunk.

All such events then would inevitably be hidden from the gods, and the fear of the people in the two lands of the Nile would follow the barge of the pharaoh, the pharaoh's gaze. The inclination of the was-sceptre of kingship would indicate a particular naked form or another worker in the reed-beds: mighty figures, the pharaoh to absorb them all - and there would then be feasts at night in the hall alone.

The cracking of backbones, the skulls splitting open and portions of flesh in wine and with spices. Power of the lord. The ka of Hor moves:

Pharaoh, alone and the sufferer of prickly heat, irritations of the skin where collars and amulets of office lie; pharaoh, plagued by insect bites and swamp fevers borne by travellers from the delta - travellers to be devoured in the city of light. Unas, alone at night, beset by nightmares of the heat, anointed; Unas, hiding from the sight of small darting animals appearing and disappearing through walls, floor and ceiling, scuttling over the sleeping chamber and between legs of guards, under tables, behind wall hangings and into pools.

Pharaoh, presented with that rarest of gifts - ephemeral and wrapped in more winding-sheets than the body of the first king, carried from the mountain top beyond the northern coast by sea; pharaoh, who had held in his hands the vanishing remnants of ice from a mountain's snow - and had smoothed his brow - pharaoh Unas once watched the sliver slip and melt away. Winds from the burning heart of the land, fiery heat of noon, dry sand blown through cracks in doors - and the snow of mountains disappeared in his hands.

Such a search for the origin of all cold. Priests in conclaves were able then to suggest every expedient: the application of flame and water, denser air - air captured above reed-bed river mouths - air of mists; the concentration of rays of the sun; the compression by weights of water alone; the extraction by distillation of pure water from the river, of water from vesicles in fishes from the Nile, of the fluid from cavities within the brains of plague victims; the exposure to chill in the desert air at night - the practice by distant tribes of the worship of snow. Snow might be glimpsed on mountain tops, would become red in the mornings and evenings and give rise to hatreds and to wars.

The presentation of small, disappearing spicules; the fragments and snowflakes, greeted solemnly and vanishing in the hand, held enviously, kept in dark caves and worshipped in haste. The speediest of rites. Ice swelling from the jar in crystals cascades onto the floor:

Shield this from the sun!

Carry this much to the pharaoh. In this, the golden vessel, and within this veil.

Pharaoh, in each of the palaces and all of the corridors. Meeting and being surprised and hopeful, stirred by the sight of more slaves than ever before, more armies in the city and the greatest work ever - the preservation of kings. In each chamber every night and where pharaoh slept amid snakes and the smaller creatures harbouring disease, there the odours from tainted, crawling plants: the smallest amounts of poison from distant regions - poison culled from plants that grow by the Nile.

As each night came, the pharaoh was assailed by wriggling small forms and snakes broader than the river: crushing palms and city walls. As each form drifted over the moon and the five-stringed harp sounded in the wind, the pharaoh cried, cast off every ornament, threw out every guard; ka-souls of night-time figures gathering about.

With every attendant eye distracted by fire, every person could ponder the worlds within worlds; worlds below the earth, worlds down communicating channels and into and out of shafts to the surface - shafts bearing light, moonlight. Down-draughts of desert air and the river flowing. This world of suffering, death, winged serpents, movement in the shade.

And the eternity in the dark gave no fewer instants stilled by fear. Each vision down paths through solid rock, the sandstone of ages - and bearing ripples - was accompanied by gentle whispers of moments caught from long ago and now the subject of speculation and of dreams, each image in these passages beneath the soil reflected secret moments to the reddened, pained eyes of the pharaoh. Instants: as supplicants and sufferers, those figures arriving after a journey and lamenting each dust-filled moment, days of sand.

We speak in whispers before our lord.

At this time the image shimmering like the point known to vanish or to contain the universe at its centre glistens. Is this the moment or another? What will join, coalesce, render itself indistinguishable from the point and prove always to have been so - what will then extend further into tomorrow and the days to follow than has ever risen in the minds of subjects, kings, the figures in temple shadows, those dazzled by the sun?

For Hor's ka was separated by the light - by motion of a white figure and the change in the warmth of days; by the movement of bright illumination, motion of winds and the circling dance of sands, by dry reeds; the swirling paths of wading birds. The small sounds that accompany walks by water at evening moved fitfully. Small abutting and connected worlds, vortices, at first close at hand, later more distant. In the passage of time when sound passed these islands, many facets to a single crystal emerged. Sound bent, refracted, became occluded or intensified and the two lands of desert, river, city and kingdom became a patchwork. Worlds: some of which connected and others which stood forever separated - or were separated at this moment and whose existence fluctuated. These became the subject of time itself.

Time which sparkled in remembered days before sickles, scythes and cultivated crops. Instants that might flicker by might cause the indrawing of breath, the momentary flutter of eyes.

Day, wind, this night, sun and moon; touch and the love of one child.

The death of the child: the swelling of lungs and the wide open mouth turned to the sky. By day and by night and the breath rising from inside. Lifting, filling, the first tremor of tongue, lips and voice. The small figure, silent and turning in the brown water below; drowned child, touch of this child. Broken limb; torn flesh, dead.

And a cry rose up, filled the throats; opened wide the mouths and caused the faces of all those present to rise: to shriek towards the sky. The cry grew above all other sounds, spread, filled every part of mother, father, any living being - and filled the air.

Birds fluttered, rose startled from reeds. Ibis and stork took flight and the figures of those huddled in the settlement, these rose in fright, looked up to where the small group reached into the reeds raising the child from the water. Cries to Osiris, dismembered god, lost.

Our loss, dream, the hope of dark nights huddled together casting about for the light in the valley. The reason why the ditches are dug after the Nile's flood: why the silt is cleared and heaped in this burning sun; the reason why aching pain is borne willingly. The fear and tearing of flesh. Oh! I see him, the child! My child, dead.

And others' hands moved the reeds aside to discover my dreams. My son's face twisted - floating among broken stems - and the mouth filled with the silt from the cataract, of eternal heat: my child!

The moment of despair is in the eyes and the movements of arms, the shoulders - and the cries throughout the village.

They carry in the air, are caught by each remembered movement so that even more than this loss, they fill the spaces between speech and gestures. Unknown in this way, an unbroken chain of fathers, mothers, sons which drifts over this desert land.

This moment persisted. Longer than the memory, longer than the lives of any then present. This grief became added to each flicker of eyebrow and movement of hand or eye raised in hope or despair. It became part of all, was known to be so derived, was recognised and all approached in this way knew what it was that so coloured the days.

And the pharaoh is set about, twisted; the pharaoh as the sufferer of all his people's grief in the night. Dreaming of the cool ice of travellers' tales, the pharaoh, his king's breath rasping at night - in the day, his divine head never turning from his people, Unas became conquered by their fears. In the face of the enemy his anger had once caused the greatest force this land had known. This pharaoh was now dying. At the meeting of the gods, at the journey along the Nile in summer from Dendera to Edfu: in the burning heat amid the people's gratitude.

The people's fear.

The relief of suffering amounted to so very much. To this divine figure was the torment of a son made known: sharply indrawn breath and the rush of water and mud chilling passages inside.

*Oh pharaoh, sufferer for all! Bear with thee, our son.
Consume our pain!*

Such recollections of the dying pharaoh preserved beyond speech or gesture became instead the way movements were henceforward to be made and still contain command, advice, endearment or chastisement. Added in this way: to the slight flexures of muscles, the inclinations of limbs and movement of eye or head that might occur in lives gathered about the banks of a river kingdom; added to these daily motions, moments of inner pain might cause a heavy movement of the hand when drawing water, a slow-paced walk up an inclined plane. Such would be known by all others around as the grief made manifest and accepted in this way were all such gestures thought to contain an inner truth and known content.

And this was truth conceived in mystery, recorded by gestures and revealing the very essence of life lived throughout ages. When once spoken at last, the very recollection of the gestured pleasure and pain made clear the way of the world's beginning. For the pharaoh left this much to his people as he died and as he progressed to the stars. The knowledge gained by the fearsome acts and the powers of the digestion of opposites: enemies and those who were strong and powerful in the land. Such manly strength and wisdom, such necessary fortitude. Unas dreams:

The ruler of the two lands: such a devout enjoyment of the flesh of men. Each sliver swallowed to increase the power of the king. The two lands and their enemies will quail at the pharaoh's name.

He dies, the vision of hands, limbs and the feet of enemies about him. Every blood-soaked swallowing motion suffered for the people of the Nile. And Unas knew of the accumulation of the powers, the growth within, and of his priests who would praise him, the devout gestures urging more, more.

Consume this small figure. This heart was worthy, this face smiled, smiled and the water closed over. Courage, it will add to every fibre.

The pharaoh lying on his bier in the delirious fever reached out for every wriggling piece of flesh: the lizard's tail, the flies on the parapet, the snakes in others' mouths. Cool, cool, the ice slivers placed on the tongue, the last fragment: this, this ice and the flesh of brave men. Ice, ice, ice. The pharaoh dies.

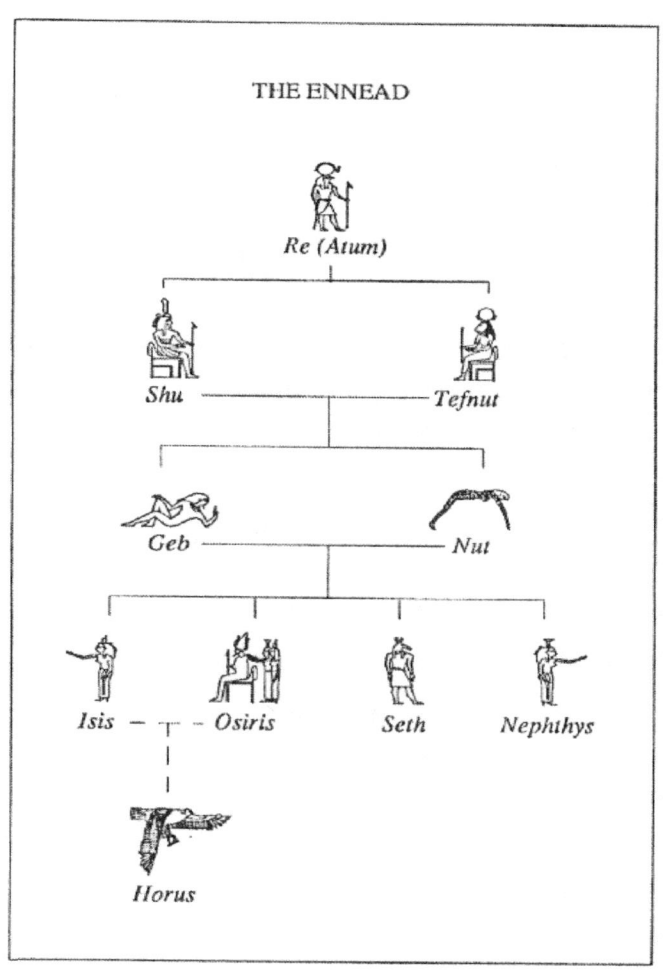

THE ENNEAD

Re (Atum)

Shu — Tefnut

Geb — Nut

Isis — Osiris   Seth   Nephthys

Horus

Chapter Three

THE GODS

The Primordial Waters and the flight of the hawk
above the gods of the Ennead.

Nighthawk, the skies in black, stars which penetrate and their images reflect in waves in the Nile.

The hawk's eye - and beneath, the talons clutch at the unbounded, at recollections down the centuries. Above Saïs, the hawk circles in flight. On the plain, reflected in water surfaces, the light from the lamps: fly, fly, the hawk!

In Saïs the sacred night - and the lights in the festival of the lamps flicker in the dark places. Devoted ones in their homes have placed these in corners, beneath the roofs, on the tops of walls and on the soil around. The night of lights and the winds move over the flames.

On distant highlands and in the valley, these lights change. Attendants of the lamps look deep into each flame: into the recollection of the light dispersed in the waters. These waters: the greater sphere around this earth, around the two lands, the Nile.

Before Re, before the form of the sun in the sky these primordial waters swirled infinitely - the formlessness, timelessness, the currents and eddies of inaction, the passive penetration by rays of light.

Throughout this ocean rays stabbed outward, inward, in all directions simultaneously. No centre, no resting place and within the Nun - primordial waters - the principle lies deep: it is Neith. Neith's birthgiving of all.

And the flights of beams of light in the ocean were to coalesce at last: one single brilliant sphere and the goddess Neith so formed the idea of birth itself. Neith of birth, and the sun-god's rays are to burn down on the earth below. A darkness, a chaos, a separation of light from the blackness and the later dark offspring: Spittle of Neith who will then threaten all.

In the city, beneath the hawk's gaze, in the wavering lamp flames lies a remembrance of the chinks and fissures - rays streaming inwards - and the light-filled ocean which surrounded all. Each lamp then to represent a portal on the Nun and the illumination outside:

See, see, the hawk. In this flickering flame, the light throughout the Nun to coalesce into the sun!

Light in all directions equally - bright and dazzling - the sun-god stirs, so on this earth when the sun daily circles: Neith of the arrows, of the bow, of the chase; mother of fruitfulness and the birth of Re!

The sun-god Re in the formless ocean alone will then create the children of Re - create the gods of the Ennead. On wings beating, the air rushes in thrusts over feathered curves and planes.

Shu, first-born son. Shu of the air, the lightness of feathers is upon your head. All souls will be grateful to you, lord of the air, for the cool wind of the north, the breezes at dawn. You are of the sun, Shu - of the rays which pour from the eyes of Re - and these, these beams will support the very heavens themselves. You are the soul of Khnemu of the First Cataract; you are the fiery heat of the sun at noon, of the sun in high summer. And oh, the journey after death! Shu, for the gods you perform the ceremony of the Opening of the Mouth with your iron knife!

Shu, you share your single divine soul with Tefnut: your sister, your wife.

Gentle rain of Tefnut, soft wind of Tefnut; the mists of the goddess over the waters of the Nile! Tefnut who will please father Re and will cause the sun-god himself to ride to the heavens: Re, to be carried by Shu - and thus the god of the air supports the sun-god himself.

From on high, father Re sees the god of earth, sees Geb - and in his arms too, Re sees beauty - it is the goddess Nut. Turn, turn the hawk: the children of Shu and of Tefnut in their embrace! And father Shu then saw for the first time the love between Geb and his daughter Nut.

Oh Nut, your naked form. The stars upon your body are before the eyes of the gods themselves!

Dark night, bright stars. All who look upon Nut's beauty desire the goddess. Geb of the earth rise up, rise up!

Goose-god Geb, the serpents coil in the earth down fragmentary paths and among rocks and boulders - where rivers from the sky might fall, pass between sands and rippling, vanish completely. It is then that your wife,

Nut, will bring forth the Great Egg of the Bennu bird. Bennu, you rise as the morning sun and are the ba of the great father, Re. You shine each morning from the Persea tree. Rays of the sun in the morning and your wings reflect all. Bennu, you renew yourself every day.

Circling about Shu, the hawk from afar sees the loving embrace. Shu looks with envy, lust and anger upon the entwined forms: Geb and Nut held close. The god Shu, father Shu - Shu in desire tears Nut away, from the arms of Geb. The screams of the night goddess echo and she is held up above in the heavens. Shu, breathing hard, raises her overhead and her limbs reach down to the earth: she is to become the firmament on high, along her naked form the stars, the stars will shine. Nut of the turning planets and the comets in the far distance; each flicker of light in the sky at night! The sun at dusk will be swallowed by the beauty of the skies and Nut you will give birth to the sun each morning at dawn!

Oh Geb, rise up to the sky. Love for Nut: your great love will bring forth the children of the earth and the children of the sky, there will be the lord Osiris, splendour of the green god of the Atef crown and the blood-red Seth, too - and Isis and Nephthys, loving sisters to them both.

But Shu loved Nut also and thus was to come about the most fearsome event of all. For love, in the greatest moment of desire there could ever be, Geb and Nut were torn apart forever and the earth and sky straightaway divided, the chasm then gaped.

In this way the love of Shu for Nut was to separate her from Geb: and the kingdom of the two lands was thus to

become fruitful and it was then that the Nile could flow
to the sea.

Mother Nut, whose body arches over the earth: Nut,
who is now the sky, protect your first-born, Osiris. Oh
sorrows of Nut: your unhappiness, your son!

The great god Osiris beloved of all Egypt and the death
of Osiris, dismembered king! Osiris, lord of the
Underworld, re-birth, and of grain. Osiris: lord of the
emmer growing in the sun by the Nile. Osiris you are
celebrated at Saïs in the festival of the lamps!

Grieve Nut, for the horror of the birth of Seth, your
son. Oh sorrows of Nut! There are tearing motions,
unnatural cries; the ferocious screams and the release
into the world of the red god in anger! Rage, rage! The
god of the desert places, the anger of chaos and of the
death of all ordered growth. The rocks will resound to
the cries of Seth. Seth, roaring in the heat of the sun: the
tearing, breaking, destroying. Twisted limbs, broken
bones: the backbone torn from the body; and evil in the
eye.

The god's anger and the cries of mother Nut. Can any
fear or joy assuage the tempers of the god? Osiris, green
god of sap rising, all changes and the conflict and the
outcome are to be recorded in this desert kingdom of the
two lands. The pain and its outcome will twist and turn
throughout the lives of those near to the river, to the
cataracts and rising rocky cliffs; those near to the slow
drift of silt to the delta. In every flicker of hand and eye
is to be seen the gesture of the greatest fear: anger,
conflict and the conquest of all. The life after life of

Osiris, lord! Neither the sun-god, Re, on high nor the mists and the swirling currents of air; nor the space above the earth and the depths of rocky soil and cliffs burnt in the sun - none, none at all would be able to save the life of the god of growth in green stems by the Nile.

The sorrowing sisters: broken life of Isis and of Nephthys - lovers to the gods. Shu, turn in the air above! Below there is an echo in the earth: lord Geb, the deed fractures the rocks beneath! The air above churns, in the anguish of a mother's love. Cry, cry, to the heavens, oh love of Shu, of Geb and the glance of Re!

Nut, your children: death in the heart, there is treachery indeed. The wife of Seth and the wife of Osiris are to tremble and to grieve. Nephthys, Isis! The god Seth rages. Red stars turn in the sky at night.

Isis, great-of-magic, death will not kill your love for Osiris, lord. Nephthys, wife of Seth, will conceal you and your child from the wrath of the god. Osiris, on his bier will there be attended by Anubis of the funerary rights - and at each end, with eternity in their hands, the sisters will kneel to honour their lord.

Jackal-headed Anubis, son of Seth - and the hawk, Horus, son of Osiris look to the ancestor gods that went before. The Ennead then: the nine gods. The creator, Re; and his children, Shu and Tefnut; and theirs, Geb and Nut of earth and sky. And the killer, Seth, and the god of the Underworld: Osiris, lord. And their sisters, Isis and Nephthys - lovers to them both.

The god Re, progenitor of all. Re, in excess of fervour reaches with trembling knife towards the erect divine member - Re reaches, cuts, and the blood flows.

Glistening in the light, blood then falls from the phallus of Re!

The heart of Re, blood of the sun-god Re! The member of Re, erect, bleeds, bleeds! Divine drops descend: they are Sia and Hu.

The drops sparkle in the light shining from the face of the lord. They reflect the god's face and - flickering across it - the expression of *the perceptive mind*. They tremble and the divine breath passes over them: breath which will be forever *the authority of the word*.

Sia, such perception and Hu, such authority are to accompany Re always. Great god Hu from the blood of Re: you are the *word*, the word at which all might tremble!

Hu is thus revealed. Hu who is to become the spoken command of Ptah to the world: the word which tells the kingdom of the two lands *to be*. And the command springs forth from the perceptive mind, for the wisdom of the god - Sia - moves within the heart of Ptah, and so perpetually Sia and Hu will accompany Re: by Hu's word the dead form of the god may thus pass over the waters. Hu is then to accompany the pharaoh; Hu, to see Unas among the stars.

Sia on the right side of Re! Of the sun in the Night Barque of Re - Sia nightly sailing with Re, passing through the Underworld and into the skies; Sia, guarding papyri, will be the custodian of the achievements of the mind. Unas thus prepared and mouth-opened will pass accompanied in this splendour on his journey to the skies.

Ptah of Memphis; Ptah, beautiful of face, who fashioned the pharaohs; Ptah-who-is-under-his-moringa-tree; Ptah who is south of his wall!

Ptah, your living image: the Apis Bull. The might of the bull, vigour of the bull, the virility of the Apis Bull will be the means by which Unas rises to the realm of Re!

On earth the Apis Bull from the temple of Ptah at Memphis carries Hor to the cemetery - while under the tongue of Apis resides the image of Khepri, the beetle of the dawn.

The triad of Ptah and his consort: Ptah, Sekhmet the raging lioness; Nefertum.

Nefertum of the assessor gods at the Judgement of the Dead. Nefertum of the blossom, of perfume: the lotus in the pool, lotus of the morning; the bright rays of morning light on the blue petals rising. Nefertum, perfume, perfection.

Ptah, upright you stand and you hold the was-sceptre in your hands: Ptah at one with Tatenen and with Seker!

Tatenen, you are god of the land at Memphis submerged by the flood and rising out of the Nile, you are the soil of Egypt itself, kingdom of the two lands: the earth at one with Geb. Ptah, you are Seker-on-his-sand in the Underworld at night!

In the winds on the mountain ridge at sunset, the jackal-god, Anubis, crouches over the cemeteries of the west bank of the Nile. The rocks burned red in the setting sun's rays; the howl of the jackal echoes at sunset. In the rock-cut tombs the cries can be heard. Anubis guards the bodies of the pharaohs, he has dried in natron the body of the king.

The viscera: removed, washed, preserved in jars; and the pharaoh's mummy resides in splendour in the dark.

———————

Nephthys, alone at night with her secret desires: Nephthys in Osiris' arms, and Anubis then will be conceived. Oh rage, rage Seth for your faithless wife! Seth, red god of anger - and oh, Nephthys, mother who will then abandon her son, see, see - Anubis guards the cemeteries, patrols the rocky hillsides. Anubis strides the promontories alone at night!

Anubis, as the heat of the day disappears, the jackal's shadow flits across the rocky outcrops. Against the stars, Anubis will prepare the body of Osiris for his reign in the Underworld. Anubis, god of the funerary rights; Anubis: jackal in the night.

Hathor, lady of the west, lady of the headland at Manu, you guard the mountain top where Anubis roams, you are from the land of silence, lady of the universe, and you join the sun-god Re at the end of the day.

Lithe lady on whose head is a crown of horns your form stands out on the headland against the red of the sky - and the sistrum sounds, you are lovely as the goddess of love and you protect the necropolis of Waset. You go between the tombs in the desert and the life on the Nile - you walk among the papyrus swamps, daughter of Re.

The foreign lands are your domain and the territory of Nubia is fearful at the sound of your approach. Nubia trembles, for you will drink the blood of men.

Horus: the hawk and the kingship of the pharaoh himself. Horus, son of Isis and her lord Osiris, is to come before Geb. There will be judgement - against Seth and the son will plead for vengeance. Horus of the Delta and Seth of the Upper Nile - and when Seth blinds Horus, Hathor it will be who restores his sight with milk of the gazelle: Horus-eye, the udjat, the pharaoh's strength, the strength against Seth. Offerings at the festival of the waxing moon: the wine.

And at the festival in Saïs once more the lamps flicker and thus by their flames the fissures into the primordial Nun are recalled: light crossing and condensing; dispersing then until all attractions and repulsions become bound. In this way the origin of birth itself: the principle - principle of Neith.

Neith within the waters. Neith: cause of the eddies themselves. The random changing and spiralling forms to condense, they coalesce and the form of Re is to be beauty within the bright sphere of the sun - to emerge at last.

51

The gods come forth and the impression lies on rivers and mountains, on the waves breaking on sand at the sea. And the influence too is on the moon and the heavens, the air passing in passages throughout the earth; on the growth of plants in the delta; on the love for wife and love of son and daughter. There, the small gestures of affection and of rage, rage!

Wisdom, authority, the passage down centuries of the influence of these gods. There, the moments between the flutter of palms on the northern shore and on all waterways; between the gusts of winds and the rustle of reeds. In each flickering moment rests the heart of Isis; grief of the bright light of Re. On the tearing of limbs and at the anger of lovers abandoned; in the spaces between the roots of reeds the breath of the gods moves. There, the shift of sand in the hot winds from the south, there, the droplets distilled from the morning mists.

The colours of the land are reflected in the eye of the hawk. Winds flatten wave-tops at the delta. Over the battles of each day is the divine vision: eye of the god, the will of the son of the Judge of the Dead.

Each distributed pleasure and pain and the hawk wings flutter, thrust downward; feathers quiver. The air turns, is held in brief contact with eddies curling earthward from both wings. The kingdom, the sun at noon.

Currents circling downwards and the uprush of desert-heated air. The vapour rising from the delta and the moisture in plants passes through leaves and into cavities between fronds, from vacuoles - and this within passages of time too small to be accounted for.

The earth; and the sky above the hawk's eye displays the crescent moon in the day and the sun then passes in the heat of the day. The stars curve at night over an eastern horizon, and in the west where rocks crack in the cooling air, fissures appear and the smallest vibrations then fracture fragments into dust. Sand, the desert filled by the forms broken in every excess of heat, every difference in the light from above and reflections from below. Each grain of sand then a record of the variations of the days and nights, the shadows passing amid bright sunlight.

The passage above, of winds and the trickle of rain.

The lands move as the winds change. In the kingdom of the two lands the desert is the territory of the spirit forms. Unseen, and the whisper of the gods in the desert: Seth, Osiris, Nephthys, Isis. Montu, of war and Min of fertile love. The divinities in rock caves, in the undulations of the desert floor, in the wind and where shadows move in the heat of the day.

Horus with wings outstretched in level flight. Horus, whose blood is of the sun, who flies upward to the sun. Horus in flight over the desert land. Oh, the river in its green fringes; the Nile from the uplands - and towards the mountain tops. Hawk, see the open water in the south, the green living movements amid the branches and leaves, the dripping water; the legs, tails, wings, heads and eyes: turning, twisting, floating between the branches in silent gestures of alarm and pursuit. Warm, living flesh. All flesh in the sun, caught in the rain and sliding into lake water - darting among fronds on the bottom and near to cataracts. Hawk in the air, in the space above the kingdom, embraced by Shu in the clouds of a damp morning: Re, rising, and light passing through the mist at dawn.

The light on feathers, on wings beating.

Through filaments, the sun-rays are diffracted and in the mists of Tefnut appear in bright rainbow hues. In the sky above, higher and higher, in dark skies. Where the hawk flies to celestial heights: the darkened night sky in the day. Stars in the passage of the sun, stars on the body of Nut. In the distance limbs, tresses, the beautiful stellar form.

Over the land of Egypt; the depths beneath the sands - of Geb - and the serpents beneath.

And the kingdom of the two lands is the kingdom of Egypt - of the death of Osiris at Seth's demand, and beneath the fluttering hawk wings Isis with Nephthys seek their dismembered lord.

Anubis! Anoint these limbs. Anubis, as the sun sets and the flight of the hawk rises, the desert becomes stilled. The gods above and within the kingdom by the Nile.

All moments in time and no time at all. Fluctuations in the gods' lives, lives of men, in the origin of glances - of inattention, of loves and hatreds; each fragmentary loss, moment of desire. Unions and oppositions, reflected light from great distances, the remote concern for distortions and hopes which arise in place of indifference. All glories and gestures taking part in creation.

———————

Creation, joy; the movement, dispersal of authority; the fragmentation and growth, the sudden outpouring; the development in silent waters, the coagulation of images in dreams; the dream of all moments and origins in the divine mind. Each evolution, each concentrated point of imagination, each focussing, each region of concern - each ramification as dispersed fragments of consciousness spin onwards. These then form their own vortices: they are the authority of figures caught fleetingly in the dying light of the sun - the sun in the silent places in desert valleys and in caves.

The gods themselves. Each origin and separated identity, the circling forms of desire and aspiration, the notions of the creating mind. Each necessity and each heartfelt wish. The beginning forces, the desires of the first awakening moment. Impulses which spin onwards: generating, bringing forth the forms and features of the world.

And figures move silently in the shadows of streets illuminated by each lamp in Saïs.

Every momentary thought of Re in the Nun and in travels in the sky. The turning, twisting currents of air and the mists in clouds obscuring the light. The first needs fulfilled and Shu and Tefnut, the most insubstantial of matter: turning, fluid. The first dream of Re becomes matter alone and the air and mist bring forth the earth and the sky in their place. Each step, each care and quality, each characteristic of growth and destruction itself. There is love and devotion - and Osiris, Seth, Isis and Nephthys walk within the desert kingdom; the two lands are to arise with the mists of the Delta of the Nile. In the air above - above the marshes, cries of the marsh birds; above the fields by the river, the stones in the bright daylight of the monuments at Giza - above all, the flight, the ba of the pharaoh himself! There in the blue skies, wings dipping: the flight of the god, hawk of the Egyptian skies. Oh the light, the skies, their very selves!

And Anubis and Hathor and Sia and Hu and the gods of the earth and the gods of the skies. For Neith and every protecting deity, the concerns of Ptah disperse throughout the creation - and in the same time no time at all.

For the memory of individual pain can cause the lives of near ones to shift and the pain so measured in each movement of hand and eye thus becomes the very manner of all dialogue. Blended, becoming superimposed, becoming added - this memory then reinforces itself like waves which pass through patterns of other waves: summing and amassing. So too, the sorrows of many losses and the joys of multitudes throughout generations. These then grow so that no longer recognisable would be the greeting with raised hand nor the look pursuing the collapse of the will. In this way they would become the very moments of discourse and of all understanding itself.

Chapter Four

THE MAIDENS OF THE HOURS

*The Decans, the Unwearying Stars, the Imperishable
Stars, the Maidens of the Hours defend Re.*

Light from the stars above. The vault of millions. The
blazing, freezing, crystal lights in the sky: each
attenuated ray passing first through upper reaches amid
the sibilance of thin winds, caught by the reflecting
surfaces on water droplets and the dust particles in the
mist. Oh, the stars which travel unwearyingly, that rise in
the east, pass the zenith and are carried beyond. Between
these events the passage of the minor fragments of time,
the inmost divisions of the life of the gods themselves.
Fractions of the breath - the instant after lightning and
before thunder. Maidens await.

Each moment on the land, each broken wave by the
shore. The particles rotate and winds turn in the desert.
The columns of sand, driven circling in the dark, obscure
the light on the horizon and the brightest stars
themselves. The passage of time, the infinite series, the
ages past and the beating heart. The dark night, and the
stars complete their path on the western horizon.

The first stars. Predecessor-of-Kenmut, and Arm-of-
Orion – and all the constellations, the thirty-six decans -
are thus to mark the passage of time. They proceed

through the sky, they measure the passing moments and
descend in the west.

The Maidens with eagerness await their lord.

Unwearying Stars, and the time is marked off in this
way. Their journey below the western horizon will be
through the darkest regions: to accompany lord Re. The
nightly journey proceeds from the separation of Geb and
Nut and the first moments. Time stretches from the rise
of Tatenen out of the waters, from the rise of the sun in
the origin, first differentiation, first awareness, first
desire of the lord. Desire which gave rise to Shu and
Tefnut and which stretches unbounded to the children of
the children of Re, to their dominion of the world and to
the interstices between created forms. The Maidens'
desires.

Starlight fills such space crossing and re-crossing and
is reflected again; it picks out the curved surfaces of
bodies floating in the sky. In the night, the light causes
the sparkle in the udjat, the Horus-eye. The hawk glances
towards the heavens from the skies and towards the
mountain tops. The hawk in level flight, silent, flies in
the space beneath the stars: Horus, ka of the pharaoh, the
elevated presence.

Horus, in the air, the wingstrokes, in the night the
passage of infinite time.

––––––––––

Night in the fields of Egypt, night in the small sleeping
chambers where burrowing forms rest. The oxen in their
stalls breathe mistily and a child cries out, turns and then

is silent once more. Over the fields, the sound of ox-yokes rattling. Beasts move their feet impatiently and the wind raises ripples on the Nile, the wind swirls between bluffs and passes through draperies in the temples, lifts the corners of sacred tapestries and reveals gold and silver, the offerings to the gods. The Maidens are present in each moment of the night.

See, here is the beauty, the divine form ascending above all heads, the wonder of the night, mother of the night. Sparkling in the cold, the limbs and tresses. The clouds before the moon's face, the dark form which breathes above the land; each star becomes a moving point on the form in the heavens: Nut, mother Nut, lithe wonder above. The stars progress over the beauty of Nut.

Water in the ditches; water lies in the runnels, the conduits; in cisterns, in vases and darkened jars. The smooth and the rippled surfaces hold the image of the stars - of flickering light in the eyes.

Black Horus-eye with the moon reflected in it. The stars of the north revolve about the centre of the night: above remote icy regions the stars rotate. Never rising, never setting these stars circle near the pole: undying, the Imperishable Stars.

Oh may the paradise of the lord be in the sky at night!

All that exists between these points: the heavenly traces and the regions of the exalted. Bliss, bliss: the passage among the stars. The turning wheel: never disappearing, the permanent, the sky-borne, the territory among the stars of the pharaoh, the lord.

And to attend the goddess of the beauty of the skies are the wonders themselves: in white the fearsome presences, delicate essences; the garlanded, with hair flowing in night breezes, writhing and sliding between leaves and grains of sand, the daughters, protectors:

Slitter-of-enemy-souls, Furious, The-one-who-sees-the-beauty-of-her-lord. The twelve daughters with eyes blazing, the beauties are to pass among the minute particles in the air.

Maidens of the Hours: daughters of Re, and the passage down infinite pathways of the desires of the lord. Into every moment: the will of the lord passes among the pulses of a beating heart and the moments in an hour; their discrete needs.

About the lord Re lies every threat and danger. Every constructed thing, every rock made to guide the passage of a river flowing to the sea, each tree at the oasis in the desert with fronds beating. Oh, you Maidens, there are concerns and directives of the pharaoh in the land, the order of the god's command! The heart beats and the hawk wings flutter and the palms move irregularly to measure no time at all. The sudden gaze of the snake's eye and the movement down its whole length - of the serpent's undulation - the passage down its back during a brief period of time. The flood of the Nile approaches and the moon raises water by the smallest amount.

The movement of the stars: the infinitesimal proper motions; their return and the disturbance of their repeated arrival; the rise in the flow of the Nile, the returned season; the light varying from morning to dusk;

the turning wheel in the potter's hand; the passage in the course of day of the pyramid's shadow in the desert; the quivering of dry reeds in the wind - reeds beating against the sides of the pharaoh's barge - the accumulation of sand wind-blown against ridges and in the entranceways to tombs, in the dry places - oh, the flicker of the serpent's tongue!

Maidens!

Each threat, the spaces between things created, the recurrent fluctuations in the imaginings of Re: spaces in time when lapses occur, the incomplete order; the dream of the god subjected to the random variations of the disturbed Nun. The light paths are perturbed: the incomplete formation of the desires of the god. In each separated fragment, unconstituted, unconstructed, the disorder remains. The breaking within threatens each moment of stress, each point at which fulfilment of the divinity itself might take place - and the originator, the lawgiver, the light of the world is turned from the path of its true development. All suffering of the god, of man, of the disturbances in the world around might then emerge and the terror of the night, too: chaotic movements, the swirling winds, the dangers perceived partially - oh the night!

Maidens: dark doubts and the loss of each preferred direction, of love and the images of fond ones. Dear ones, the light touch of the mother's hand.

Each movement, and growth, and affection may be disturbed. The dark, disordered evil spreads wide and into the very depths of each smile: for the loved being; for the welcome in each indrawn breath.

Such discord discomforting the god. The anguish and the pain of sensitive moments is revealed. The crushing of the spirit, the imposed restraint denying hope. Dispersed pain that is felt at the extremities, which limits all gestures - and pain limits the hope that might direct motions of hand, eye and limb, which might constrain the very first impulse: create or die.

Thus death would creep forward at the Maidens' command: the breath and the smallest movements and the engendering act overwhelmed. The dissociation, disorder: within the fibres, the breaking, tearing; the driven thing is hurt and incapable of further motion. All energy spent, the creep of decay over walls and into rooms and the vanished inspiration of all deities. Re, the slow death of the sun.

But in the Nun was the struggle to assemble each luminous tissue: processes throughout the created world - the gods arising in their separated parts then engulf the fractured, dark parts of decay. The sun, the sun; guidance of all.

───────────

Thus the rise of chaos and the struggle of the light in the kingdom of the light. The rapid turning of the stars, the rise again and again of the sun in the desert, the briefest intervals in which conflict is enjoined and the light burns within the darkness.

And the need was to arise while Re examined all pathways equally: the desperate sense of advancing blackness. Each glance cast outward: each direction in the light of day. Above, below, to one side and the other, to each direction a glance of the sun-god, Re.

Within the daily cycle, in each hour of the night lie the twelve goddesses of the hours of the night: the priestesses of the darkness, Maidens of the Hours, the very hours themselves in caverns and beneath the earth.

Maidens: defenders of Re in the night. The enemies are in the interstices, in passages of the rock, in the flowing waters. Abandonment and the echoes of cries of chaos, the disturbed reflection of the origin and the fates themselves. In every passageway, underground where the fiercest fiends roared; where they hissed, screamed and tore at the rock itself; where they burnt their own images upon all exposed surfaces; where water boiled upon contact with their breath - there, there, were the staring eyes of disordered vision: of the fiends bleeding, suppurating; torn and fragmented. Fiends, fiends, the Maidens of the Hours must defeat each one in turn!

Each incomplete act of creation, each limb formed from a divided attention. Re! The talons - and the eyes stare, stare!

The power of the lord is dispersed and takes root everywhere. The beauty of Re emerges at night. Custodians of the gleaming light, the life of Re animates these daughters and his power, dispersed, grows in the darkness and through channels beneath the earth. Down centuries: the pursuit of the discord among the random formations of the creating lord.

Such emanations of the incomplete form of the gods. The distant concerns, desires, needs of the god. Through their eyes: the writhing, the tearing; the disturbance in time of a partial birth; the sight of each cataract in every smooth-flowing river; the collapse of rocks in heat and cold and on hill tops - and rocks move towards each other and collide, the sound reverberating in valleys and along the river.

The sound would be heard in all parts of the land. At work and in the fields; in the temples and places shaded by the pylons, pyramids, the obelisks and the statues in the desert; in the desert air, winds rising, the sound echoed - as of the five-stringed harp and the collision of the rocks - it could be heard out at sea.

On the shore, by the Delta, along the Nile and in the headlands; in Nubia, Punt, in Libya; across the sea, the sun's rays mount over the waves and the mists disperse: flights of the gulls, the light on their feathers. Among mountain tops in high winds and where the dust from the desert enters fine rivulets: Oh Maidens of the Hours disperse all! Make safe the evil in the beating of the heart; the blinking of the eye.

The time passes: such penetration through ears, eyes and mouth, through the viscera - and with the breath of kings. The sharply indrawn breath, the sigh, the rattling breath on the bed before death. Joy, the passage of the lord's time: the moments, these hours to protect the lord.

Indrawn breath and within, the air and the clouds. The stars which circle the pole and those - unwearying - which rise and set: such stars descend with the sun below the horizon from the mountain at Manu to the mount of sunrise at Bakhu. Thus the indrawn breath matches the beat of the world's time: hours, air drawn deep within.

And breathing out: the power and control of the lord's wishes; the pursuit and defeat of distant threats. In each instant - the breath of the hours - are the perils assembled. The dangers amass, the needs of the lord Re overwhelm the creation. But the Maidens, thrust out among these disturbances: the urges, the daughters of Re himself move in silence. They engulf the greatest fears, destroy them through the echoing ages - those spreading outward from the first emergence of Tatenen from the waters, from the first command of Ptah, from the first breath of Re.

Out, the urges drive towards the periphery and the moments are guarded, made safe for the lord. In the night, twelve hours, twelve caverns and the fearful evils become dispersed in this way.

———————

No moments at all. This time paused, was stilled. Developments in paths unknown and unknowable.

The stilled moments reached into the very heart. Wherever imaginings rose or lost their significance: of grief or affection; such moments as these became supported by contact with forms gesturing, and these figures with yet others - a web which spread outward, at times in darkness - and the sharply indrawn breath of expectation whispered in the depths of night too. Thus the gatherings of small groups took place in dwelling places in silence – and these spread from certain swelling moments and became the origin and reflection of all instants experienced in pain. While speech itself might fail, be limited by the strangeness felt on first contact with others' tears; these gestured moments of emotion and pain were cast outward, and returning inward, joined other instants to the wealth of indications around. Signs that went before - there were those faithfully expected, and others that were hoped for. There were those indications known about, felt by others now absent; and yet others felt by those known continuously for years in separated parts of the land.

Each instant in time realized during this desert moment. This fear by the river, pain by the river, death of the son; the loss, last moment, lost moment; death of a son.

Chapter Five

MIN

Rain. The god Min appears in the desert.

The power that existed, persisted from those years of desert nights, before pyramids, the pharaoh, the two lands, this kingdom of the Nile. Before the tilling of soil at all, while the Nile at flood simply drowned and starved men. In those days men knew of power.

Power which gave rise to stars, which made plants grow in profusion, women fruitful and the river to merge forcefully with the sea - which dried the skin under sun's rays and made the wind move against cliffs: sandstone, rocky, fragmented, fractured.

What power in the land! What heat in the sun. Was this the power to be seen in the desert - when glinting in the unaccustomed way - the rains fell? At the limit of vision the sparkle of droplets. On the surfaces of rocks the drops first pass to vapour then wet exposed surfaces. In the bright hues of the desert sky the drops glisten and where winds have driven hard sand against rock outcrops at last, the pattern among splashing drops becomes disturbed; a vortex, a solid surface where only air would seem to be.

In the descent of rain an outline invisible except where drops splash intercepted in mid-flight. Invisible, the form revealed by the rain of a thousand years, rain in the heated air, rain in bright sunshine, rain from cloudless skies, rain for certain eyes alone, rain in the desert.

The traveller's vision over dunes and when the whirlwind of heated air circles; dry, the wind burned. In the desert steaming droplets fell and coalesced from a blue, clear sky. They swirled, drove in waves, wet hands, face, linen, sandals, the hides of beasts and wet all surfaces; they covered the skin.

But the surface with no form beneath glistened too. What shape in the desert? First the air just above the sand where the steam rose as the droplets fell. In this region, at first discernible against the rising clouds of vapour: the two straight and vertical shapes - with the sand visible through them; then the larger form above, moving, *breathing,* and the sight of the horizon glimmering through the wetness suspended in the air. Above, the two diaphanous forms flowing in the breeze: feathers above where the eyes, mouth and head appear. Transparent, the vision of the being that stood higher than any man, taller than temple walls at Waset, than the tallest pillar, glistening now completely transparent: an invisible form picked out only in the rain drops running together, running in rivulets over shoulders from one upraised arm, dripping from the end of the invisible flail held in the wind; moving slightly in the wind and fearsome to behold. That the desert might be peopled in this way, invisibly, fearsomely - by figures in the sand, among the dunes and broken rock. Unknown, unrecorded, unrecognised; not worshipped, given no sacrifice, subject to no placation and looming above all heads: the unseen form.

Rain, rain in the desert is the transformer, that which makes the unseen seen: the driving, swirling mists of droplets, vapour; the mists curling up calves; the heaving chest - and condensing, dripping from every extended form.

What majesty is this? What command, what rigid, forceful, demand is this? Who will be transformed, transfixed, rendered complete by the image that is not seen? The figure erect, visible as the transparent space between the wet surfaces of unseen forearm, unseen thigh: this commanding, unseen erect phallus in the hand, phallus in the desert wet with the rain, visible only as a greater transparency in clouds of vapour in the desert - a vortex and made visible at last. The god's figure, god's need, god's demand?

Name yourself, invisible figure of the sands and rain!

The storm departed. The sun burned onto sand and rock outcrops. Rivulets trickled dry. Patches of dry surface on rock between puddles where water film had been. In the desert sun the puddles dry. Green and brown deposits on rims decreasing inwards. Water hissing and boiling now in its moment before vanishing, and above the sands almost no detail at all of the unseen god remains.

There! He is there invisible now, completely. There, the impression of his feet, and the occasional dry eddy of windblown sand marks the limbs, but still; not marked against the horizon. The sun visible through chest, head and upraised arm, nothing now betrays the presence of the silent figure of the open air. The god no more.

And travellers might become prostrate to the empty air. This desert of the east, peopled in such a way! Towards the horizon where rocks standing above the sand become separated by the heated air, rising to the blue of the sky. In this land - here and here - the figure again; another there, the desert alive: an invisible city too terrible to imagine too difficult to see.

Run to the small people in the valley, to the drawers of water, the concubines and the minor officials, run to the friends left for just one afternoon. Bear the image; warn, call for reconciliation, describe haltingly, gesture fearsomely, the fearful shape. Indicate those buildings that might reach upwards to the waist, those where the feathers and headdress might be, show the feet - spread wide - move the chest in the manner of the divine breath, give cause for alarm; run to priests and the representatives of the pharaoh, of Horus, and those workers in the temple, show the hand about the phallus, the breath of the god, the god's demand. What god is this?

Word of this might so spread about the land. Amid the turbulence at the cataracts the description is whispered of the unknown figure of the open air and in the noise of the water forcing passages through rocks in the riverbeds, in between these rippling sounds, whispers become mingled. Pauses then permit the interruption of these gurgles, trickles, the roar of water falling from the greatest height, so that all recounting of the tale, all recollection of the vision becomes adjusted to these sounds.

Pauses then in speech, interruptions in the tale indicated by the upraised hand, the mouth opened, the arm raised, the eye following the horizon, the look fixed into the darkness. All movements so pressed to ensure the recollection of the tale amid the sounds of the southern land become in this way vital to the tale, necessary for the proper pronunciation of each syllable, the necessary partner to sounds of the name of the nameless god.

In the fear of those wishing only to avoid the terror in the desert to the east, in the anxiety then for whatever hidden forms might assail travellers there, these breaks and pauses suggest all manner of fears; become the words in a language of similar darknesses. Wherever the flow of speech might later become interrupted, the question - *Is this mention of the lord?* - becomes framed in doubting minds or knowing ones inserting such silences into speech to bring about the fear so desired: the recollection of the sudden mists - the unknown figure of the open air.

Pauses and gestures. In this way the web of discourse: stretching to primordial days before the first pharaoh, when speech rose only from the sounds of animals and the winds around.

Chapter Six

HOR'S TOMB

Funerary rites, Meretseger concealed, the serpents and the akh-soul.

Erect, the figure of Hor is to be approached by the priest of Ptah-Tatenen, the maker, creator, the great god of the Mound. The form of the man, prepared and mouth-opened: the journey now to the Field of Reeds.

Anointed, made perfect for this journey, supported vertically, the upright totem: triumph of Osiris, the stable, erect, djed-column itself. Erect from the single final agony, Hor is now saved in natron; the jars: Hapy, Imsety, Duamutef and Qebehsenuef - sons of Horus - and the lungs, liver, stomach and entrails are so preserved.

In the necropolis at Memphis, the snakes await. In the soil broken from the desiccating sun, in cracks through stonework and masonry: the only passage possible - that of the uraeus, the cobra - coiled, living in coolness, darkness; supplied in life by the agonies of men. The coiling forms wait.

In the heat of evening the procession - perfumed, awaiting the judgement of Osiris, fearful of Amemet, hopefully submissive to Maat, and examining congruencies: those within the life of Hor, the wishes of the pharaoh, divine one Horus - and wisdom shared with Thoth.

The servant of the god placed close to the anointed - and the sun-god will look upon his subject:

Re, from the Solar Barque look down to your nightly struggle against the Serpent: look down on the fate awaiting the servant's desire.

The last closing of the tomb's entrance, the last flicker of light - and then all is gone. Alone, the odour of sandalwood grave goods, of shabti-figures in cedar from Gubla - of Osiris' rest. Alone and silent in the dark kingdom. Now the destruction, now the decay.

In fields by the river, the cry of the ibis - great god Thoth - and the wind in the rushes and the cry of small birds disturbed by danger in the grass: the flicker of tongue tasting the air from the delta, the aromas of soil, decay of vegetation dried in the baking sun. The nest of vipers, the solitary cobra: the great serpent Meretseger moves among long grass and feels the sound of sickles harvesting reeds.

In the necropolis the noon sun burns rocks which crack and flake in no shade at all, dries the wisps of grasses and desiccates seeds blown into crevices. The shadows are dispelled from the sculptured faces: Anubis, Osiris, Thoth, Horus-the-pharaoh. The sand drives hard against the tomb entrance, a small patch of shade, and in there the black coils slightly move. As the sun sinks into the desert and the winds rise; the small air movement drifts from the interior humid with sandalwood, natron, oils, the libation, the final meal. The tongue flicks outwards and the eyes stare. The blackness ahead now no longer simply shade: the origin of slight odours distinct from the desert - and the snake creeps forward, disappears between rocks and descends from view.

In the dark, its fellows. The coffin now glistens in the small light from above. The serpent-mound reaching towards its head shivers and writhes, moves slowly and then engulfs the head, mouth, eyes, the body of Hor. It can be seen tearing at the cartonnage, bandages, the mask in death - and penetrating the eyes. Each snake disappears within. Flesh creeps.

No snake may hear the sounds from the desert, the lamentations for the death of the child in the river; the wind in leaves overhead. But through the skin and scales and into these serpents' bones come those other tremors which vibrate when the man is named, the god is named, when the place of Osiris' rest is indicated; where thirteen-fold burial brings forth Hapi, the Nile, and the fourteenth is cherished, caressed, desired by Isis; is erect, is dead, will fulfil every need as the unseen god amid rain in the desert might do, will give to the two lands their ruler, will bring about the avenger, the son, the rightful heir.

Horus, falcon king, reigns in these lands and in the temple in silent obeisance, Hor, priest of Montu, would pour his libation to the pharaoh and Horus at one, indivisible. The true son of the true son, and the snakes might wait for their fill and so attend to no part of the development of this sound screamed to the sky - *The death of my son!* - and silent thoughts unspoken throughout all time then take their shape. The gestures increase, the silences shrink, grow, have their meaning, and the vibration of sounds that other creatures hear, these too produce their most delicate discourse. But for that other serpent, Apopis - coils about Atum; coils within the Nun - the serpent, Apopis, is unhearing and unheard.

Blood, the serpent sucks blood. The head of Meretseger, raised, hooded - and the eyes transfixed. From the fangs drop the cold blood of the corpse: after natron has dried the flesh, after viscera are removed and stored in jars - Hapy, Imsety, Duamutef and Qebehsenuef - after these a residue.

The serpent and the lesser snakes coiled angrily raise their heads from the chest of Hor, look up from the eyes of Hor and wriggle down inside Hor - to the legs, the feet, hands, back and waist. The snakes who become Hor:

Hidden, we descend and we live, preserved, hardly breathing at all. We thrive on one man's final agony. We stir as the ages pass. We move as stars, sun and moon move. Great Re, you sail in your solar barque and you strive against the serpent of the Underworld, Apopis. Each day you rise, great Khepri, The Becoming, Re in his form at dawn, and you sink to the western horizon, great Atum-Re and we, in the remains of the final pain stir only slightly under the flesh. The years pass.

Secure we hope for Becoming, to transcend this state and we who feed on the flesh seek our condensation from the dispersed. Will our efforts find success? This tearing, gorging, writhing; this feeling once as he did - constrained within limbs, rigid yet able to move, to run, climb, walk fast or rest; to think, see, hope and love. These desires, our desires, and we seek for transformation towards the light, we seek to embrace that which all serpents fear; the open clear light from above; bright day, the open air.

The unknown figure of the open air: what life, demands and what transformations there have been! What figure is this that we must emulate? With this figure into the light, to twist and turn in delight, float from the earth, rise dispersed in air, float in mists; to dispel rising dew; to rise above the circling insects, birds, the coils of the heated desert air, float above sounds of trickling sand.

And the rays will penetrate the body, will enter upwards, downwards, from the western horizon and the east. This spirit-form transforming, this akh: heat and light in every direction. Penetrating the body - limbed - the head, eyes and mouth and passing through to emerge, to light, sparkle, radiate in every direction, to become like the sun.

Above Tefnut the mists supported in the unbounded way, in space, great god Shu in infinite light, in unending space we glisten, we radiate among ourselves, separate and communicating still, suspended, joyful. There is no height and no depth, there is no direction at all and we feel no weight, no wind, breath, no air. Our forms transformed, no

76

shape at all. No extension, no breadth or height to these points of light.

———————

Brilliants, in the bright space we communicate, hold each other close or far apart. A light-filled web and rays penetrate all. What communication is this that passes between spicules, ice crystals, points in such light? One thousand reflections and the light so changed takes on all colours. Red, yellow, blue. There are no directions picked out by crystals suspended in air and transfixed by light. Each turns, receives light, alters rays and colours and passes light on. Light so moved will become directed otherwise, to sparkle in different crystals suspended in the air; turning, changing colours in this way - the rainbow above the earth, above Hapi, the Nile, above the pharaoh's endeavours, death in the river, the serpents' lair.

Chapter Seven

NEFERTUM

City of pain. The still pond where the lotus blooms.
The groves.

Serpents. Atum, the dying form of the sun-god descends towards the horizon. Atum-Re, pro-genitor, alone in the primordial waters of Nun, proceed to the lion, Aker, enter the Underworld, enter the Duat!

The hours. The hours of night and the cries of night birds at each disturbance and the sounds of jackals and the hippopotamus in the water, the calls of all animals awake; movements of the smallest insects on stone walls, on tapestries, the surface of bronzes, the jars, amulets, crowns of the upper land and lower kingdom. Heat in the night, cries of night birds; there is fear and there are thanks for the smallest cry from across the water; Hathor in the fields, Thoth in the reeds, Sobek in the water.

Abroad, more silent movement occurs in the temple precinct: the sleeping man moves fitfully evading the terror of the dream.

The boats drawn up in the river are lapped by the Nile, as the wind rises the desert air, swept up, moves towards the city and flies into streets with sand to sting faces, dry the skin, mouth and eyes; it is then the strange tales of travellers and emissaries, the punctuated, gestured reports of merchants and seamen give rise also to desires. The hours.

Dearest wishes, the moments, free from all anguish, which enter in the night, pass between the rocking motions of the boat, the cry of the marsh birds; the gentle pressure of fingers against the palm. Wishes which unite the slightest, furthest, most different and the silent. To hope, to know what might at all times befall the greater aspiration, the greater desire.

The two lands represented in this way: the desires of labourers in fields and maids in service to unwilling lords; the scribes and pupils who whisper suppressed desires, that fill waking moments between the arousal at dawn and first food of the day, between the draughts of emmer beer and water from the Nile.

Hold this dear! Whatever may be seen. The moment of time within time, the future now, the light in the city in dreams.

The dream is of green grasses in dew and this will come to be, the hope is of the recording of all anguish in the finer recesses: the city of pain.

Cry! To the crystal pylons in unbearable heat. Cry, the figures moving in the distant broad streets - seen above city walls in palaces between columns, gateways; in repositories and on battle fields, where water flows in the desert. By the sea, above the clouds, above rock outcrops, above torrents; in gardens.

Gardens of suffering and gardens of desire. The figures ascending: into rock groves, into shade. Light passing through leaves, passing to sheltered ground. In these groves all suffered pain to be spoken aloud, shouted; all loss and vanished hope called out: the name of this suffering is spoken into the mouths of caves. Beneath these trees every other pain. By the stream, in whirlpools by lotus ponds and where the lotus ascends, the sun rises. The lotus opens. Day begins and spreads perfume of Nefertum:

Oh god, Nefertum! So greatly to be desired: hope of my hope, true light of true light.

Suffering will be charged, changed, sweetened. No more the pain, and the figures beckon among themselves. A call, not spoken; composed of the small inflections of arms, hands, limbs and face, and within the god's sight a gathering: the rippled movement outward down paths through these groves. The same gestures seen through palm fronds and in sheltered spots by rocks, by the stream on the side of hills or at other small depressions.

Crowds then move forward and congregate passing among others still engaged in daily gestures of gathering food and preparing for sleep. But through this throng the notion passed; gathered to itself the solitary figures on promontories, those engaged in preparing bread, in lifting up pitchers, pouring wine and numbering the dead. Through the far reaches of the throng the flicker of recognition passes and among those who remain, there are gestures of regret, the reluctance to stay still, the inability to stay silent. The figures make their way to regions not yet visible: clouded, obscured, they enter one by one, eventually only a single gesturing arm remaining – or a leg or lower back. Each is sustained momentarily and the movements preserved in this way are to be remembered, joined with other residues of gestures so to form the silent message: the idea preserved and now growing; the hope for the future without dreams.

No dreams at all and the lotus rises; to the light, the air, the rays of the sun. From depths; the bloom and the soul of Re in the small space, in secret, amid green fronds and the dappled light; sun on the water, leaves on the water, the great god and origin of all. Of sons of Horus: of the gods of this flower. Bloom in the growing light, bloom in the gentle warmth and ripples over water: the dark depths, the water's night. Rise God Re, lotus, beginning and creator of all. Perfume of Nefertum rise from deep water.

This origin, this small clearing, these sun's rays. Here all labour of all mankind, all hopes and the deeds of gods and men, here the desert and the origin of lands: the death and pain of all. Perfume of Nefertum penetrates all.

Oh lotus belonging to the semblance of Nefertum, I am the Man. I know your name, I know your names, you gods, you lords of the realms of the dead, for I am one of you. May you grant that I see the gods who lead the Underworld, may there be given to me a seat in the realm of the dead in the presence of the lords of the west, may I take my place in the Sacred Land, may I receive offerings in the presence of the lords of eternity, may my soul go forth to every place that it desires, without being held back from the presence of the Great Ennead.

The cries echo into cave mouths and down tunnels in solid rock. The lotus blooms. Each form of a man thus

81

disturbed rises, makes his gestures and the pain becomes dispersed. On the still pond a slight ripple, in the leaves by the bank the slightest of tremors. The sunlight on the water glowing, on the bank small eyes among the leaves. Steamy heat, silence, the mist swirling among dark vegetation, flowers.

Bloom, rise, origin of all! This awareness in the dappled lake: in this silent reach all pain, the knowledge in this city, in this grove; the gestured forbearance and dreams among the figures in the garden of suffering and the garden of desires.

The petals open, perfume of Nefertum. Oh secret, secret!

Bloom, rise, and in the waterways where earthworks open - darkness. The water trembles silently and the ripples pass to the flower.

To hope, to love all reaches of this Nile. These water rises, these fecundations; the rise of vegetation, of crops. Great god Osiris, your renewal amid the heat, the birth among rushes, the growth of the kingdom, the life amid deserts: the deposition and recording of the language of desires. Oh god of all awakening, god of all fathers; suffering, this land. Rise now.

In small unobserved moments the petals rise to open in the light.

The language of gestures: arms, shoulders, legs, the face. The flicker of recognition could be seen in each figure passing in the gardens and through the groves:

We know how pain coalesces, joins these happinesses and brings forth the cry. The raised arm. To fill these hours and days, to form the gentlest recollections; to cause the conceits of power to grow; to join efforts in all types of adversity and to speak of love between ourselves.

From the cry for danger, for food and love the figures will hope and cherish, protect and save. In these deserts now, able to conquer, believe and recollect our mysteries, what future will grow?

And from the past such images! At one moment the origin of pain to be recollected; the exercise of funerary rights; the origin of rain in the desert, snowflakes on mountain tops; the judgement of travellers' lives. Oh bright specular futures, the winds!

Winds in the leaves of palm trees and on the white wave tops of the sea. The wind over the sand rising from the shore and carrying with it fragrances of distant lands. To feel their presence, to hear carried on each eddy the echoes of distant lives.

We are unsatisfied without the wonder of stars above and the images of gods to accompany us.

Among the stars the space to be filled trembles at the approach. That all might exist. All those ideas developed in recesses where the air is heavy with sandalwood, cedar wood; in the light flickering by the cave mouth, and where talk occurs in whispers. The changes that may be made: those elements requiring adjustment - and the sky and stars wait above.

We know we can perform the rarest of feats. Command our endeavour, commend the journey. The limitations cease: this flight above desert winds, the still air, the turning air.

With this passage to the upper air, the figures in the gardens and within groves rise up. The figures bend towards their fellows, indicate the order of their own desires and pass in silence into passages in the rocks, into caves. They descend dark corridors and then return.

The language will fade away, these ideas may then fill the space, the air above the god in thunder, god in rain, god in the desert.

The figure will move through emptiness. Suspended above the ground, in the heated air; over the stone floor; above votive pediments and the displays of water in a parched land. The figure unbounded and moving through doorways and into corridors, perhaps by the gentle motion of draughts alone.

In the light of stars the shimmer of gossamer; the reflected light from the stone surfaces of jackal, ibis, crocodile and baboon. The figure in flight, in thin air - to drift in the movement of the air.

In the corridors and by the temple, inscribed images flicker on walls in the dim light, between shadows as the form drifts by. The gentle passage of the suspended figure; no contact at all, the figure in the city formed in the night.

See these forms, in the moonlight, in the glades, in caves. In the night. Stars, circling the pole - bright remnants of moments in the two lands, to be visualised during the passage towards every cave. This garden, illuminated in silver. Light from the moon.

The low shrubs and green expanse now appear grey.

Grains blow from the desert. Hope for transformation into this other life which might be known and felt. The other cares and dreams: the visions down corridors and within alcoves.

Shade - heat rising in the sky - and from the water mist rises to the moon. Shining eye of Horus. Suffering figure of the open air - visible only in the light blocked and broken by the shift of large wings, the movement of the figure in the night.

Over the fields at the margin of the river, over cornerstones and the elevated channels where water glints in the moon's light, over these the draperies wave - of linen, of gold thread and silver. They lift and flutter in the warm breeze from the night-time desert. Air above the fields rises, there is the scent of mud-caked flowers, emmer; the sound of animals tethered. Forms below in darkened rock recesses, familiar domestic beasts and the presence of those beings from the life after life; ba-souls - of the mood, direction of life and the ruling principles - Maat and Wisdom; presence of birds.

The wild calls fall away - to darkness - to the stars that burn, turn, arise and disappear. But these northern stars, these Imperishable Stars, these images will circle, will never set. They are the sacred, sanctified remnants of lives completed amid heat, sand, the passage of the Nile.

From on high these lives may continue. In the city, in crossing places where moonlight, starlight and the drift of warm winds penetrate, in this darkened vale the darkest, blackest image of all.

What aspiration, to dwell among the stars! Will there be cold, and winds, air, love, companionship too? Will there be hope in such heights to bring forth secrets forever - now the source of this struggle. To lift and rise! In this manner the stars.

Desire when the Nile floods pass into every fissure.

Oh what will it be like to live at last among the stars?

The moments become preserved. We feel, we feel! Each instant recollected in delight: caught, displayed, made the substance of the dream.

To the recollections of childhood can be added moments when desires met and coalesced. The movement as one. All adventures then to be present in the northern sky: moments remembered fondly; lives remembered so - in these stars - not dipping, stopping, giving rise to any change.

These northern stars turn above, they are visible at all nights in the desert. Some relief exists for crestfallen men, for those seeking to hide from their destiny; the defeated, broken and uncertain. The deep; at each level joy and men's suffering to be represented. Such architecture of the abyss will hold all dreams and all despair.

Figures beneath us, beneath the surface, desert surface, struggling and dreaming.

The origin is in the unspeaking moments, wordless years, silent ages in caves by the Nile, the nights under the stars: brutish, uncomprehending; nights given to fears and dangers and the growing unspoken needs.

On each inward sloping side the abyss might show regions where pain and joy would intersect. And at the greatest depth, this visible point: the pole itself. For the rest, the happy intersection of desert ruin and upper heavens might obscure all.

THE FORMS TAKEN BY THE
SUN GOD DAILY

Re

DAY

Atum

SUNSET   DAWN

Khepri

NIGHT

Flesh-of-Re

Chapter Eight

THE ENTRANCE TO THE DUAT

*The first hour of the night-time journey, Atum becomes
Flesh-of-Re, the water-dance.*

The journey of Re in the daytime sky and in the
Underworld: Re-in-your-name-of-Atum descends to the
horizon. Bright, the dying red rays of the sun-god, the
rays burning onto the papyrus-head prow, the stern, the
large timbers. This dying vision of the day, the light
penetrating tall figures always present too; the
companions of the barque, companions of the god,
travellers towards the night, righteous forms, light forms:
silhouettes and attributes illuminated by the bright sun
itself.

To the gap in the mountains, to Manu, the red
luminescence is visible through all outlines, each feature:
the naos-canopy on the Barque of Re, oars each now
transparent to the light; heated columns rising from the
desert air.

From the cave tombs in the west the figures mass. As
each man's double in life, his ka moves from the sealed
doors of the tombs; as each ka, in fact, *comes forth in the
day* to walk unseen among living men; as each akh - the
light, active principle upon death - rises, moves away; as
the bodies themselves, the khats, lie preserved in their

tombs - as these elements diverge, the bas, the souls of motion, flutter wings in the sunset, and these bird-forms with the heads of men and women mass for their solar lord. They are the sons, fathers, the soldiers dead in battle, the boys drowned and the mothers dead in childbirth.

There have been crimes and disappointments and there have been hopes, conceit and the calculation of small advantages; each then moving silently, unseen, above hot desert sands in the haze of the heated air.

And the priests have prepared the khat of each man. The bodies have been washed, reamed, dried, anointed, wrapped; granted shabti-figures, scarabs; granted the texts of the passes to all gates, guardians, all caverns of the night - texts against the serpent, Apopis; texts for the Underworld, the Duat; for Osiris, king of the dead. Spells against the second death, against annihilation in unseen cavities, against these lost ones' torments; for the life of light with the sun, in happiness and with all desires intact. Continuation, the journey greatly to be desired; the aspiration of dead ones by the Nile.

The ba-souls assemble in the light of the descending sun. Hor's ba flies where a boy, dead in the Nile, and where Unas the pharaoh had once passed - and the centuries too had then passed and the dynasties too.

And Hor's ka, Hor's double has walked from the tomb.

Light strikes out to the caves in Manu, to the realm of Meretseger once wrapped round the mountain top - slithering, the scaled form caught in the dying sun's rays, Meretseger coiled round tree and cave mouth; the dweller within Hor.

Here the waters of Nun meet the unseen river, River of Urnes, river of the Underworld, river of the Duat. Here the sun-god descends to earth, here in the crimson glow the transformation itself - and the barque, Sektet, is heated in these burning rays. The scorched timbers are lapped by waters made boiling by this bright presence of Atum. Red, the dying sun.

The ba-souls assemble on rocky prominences, they make obeisance; the sun burns, the water steams in this intense light, all features become indistinct. The god's head: a blinding luminescence that cannot be seen, all are transfixed in the light. Now in this region before the Underworld, in this reddened, parched, rocky hollow, among these caves where the boiling river carries the scorched barque - timbers splintering, the dark wood charring - here the brightness becomes greatest of all. Here - the ba-souls' vision - and the attendants of the god clear the last fading trace of the living presence of the solar lord. Re-in-his-name-of-Atum is transformed.

In the indistinct brightness burning down on the rocks, in the centre a *dead* light will emanate from the form of the sun-god: Flesh-of-Re, and in the very middle of this illumination, the erect god, ram-headed god, source of heat and light, the fearsome horned god of the night will now move indistinctly within the bright image. The day deserted.

The rocks are cracked and scalded by the nightly arrival of this radiance. The dead light, dead.

And oh, this form of the lord, the Flesh-of-Re; this god of death entering the Duat. The river boils and hisses, cools the rocks, cascades from the skies, whirls in vast currents, and pulls at the vessel. All about the ba-souls assemble. The god's helpers: Sia, Hu, The Steersman. Tall figures and the light burns through them. The bright rays pass through their flesh undiminished: figures on the barque. The Flesh-of-Re is upright, ba-souls move forward and his figure is embraced by the serpent, Mehen, protector. The vessel is prepared for the journey on the River of Urnes, the journey through the Duat.

The ba-souls of the newly dead will approach this barque, plead with the god, plead for acceptance. Even now winged figures of ba-souls can be seen on this vessel to accompany the gods.

To travel with Flesh-of-Re, to pass nightly with Flesh-of-Re, to be safe with The Flesh, to spurn dangers and horrors, enter the night-time world, pass through the gates, enter the caverns, pass the dark hours amid the illuminated ba-souls of early gods from the days before the language: the ba-souls of Pe and Nekhen, spirits from before these hopes and fears. Amid these revived ones, other prostrate souls cry out, their bodies reamed, preserved; in bindings - viscera held by Hapy, Imsety, Duamutef and Qebehsenuef the four sons of Horus - amid these the cry rings out, they shriek as the sun sets:

Save, Save, Flesh-of-Re, great god!

The bright saving light then moves on. Can such forms be redeemed? Can such loved ones be restored - and this, this dear one possessed of each name and opening motif; this one with each formula; this dear one equipped for the opening of the gates, the opening of the ways; with this one the safe passage, the preserved journey - and this form so passes broken remnants, fading residues. The remains, all origins.

Egypt, the life in caves and the howl of beasts in the dark. Rise, rise in this night; to these stars, this sun, moon, the rain in the desert; earth-god, mother, all faith and belief and the origin of love and hope. Preserve, save the dear one. Cry, cry to the great god:

Flesh-of-Re, preserve, give safe passage for we tremble, we fear.

The Duat opens. In the dark recesses apes labour: they draw back the gates. Distant singing is heard. The darkness is stabbed by jets of fire, by moving pools of light.

From each crevice and ledge, from each side channel, from behind each boulder the swaying, fire-spitting, hooded cobras rise, hiss their welcome, give light to the dead god, Flesh-of-Re. They illuminate the gates first and their burning pools spill down, cascade from rocks overhead, fall to sand at the foot of the cave, fall to the river surface and so boil there; they hiss and the fire burns even below the water. Shadows creep back to the recesses of the cave of the first hour of the night.

Oh Maidens of the Hours: The Daughter-of-Mut, The Raiser, The Goddess-of-sickness; sing, give praise, protect! The adorers bend low on either bank, the Barque of Re moves forward. In the distance the vessel is preceded by images: the forms of Re - by the dying sun, Atum; by the scarab, Khepri, god of the sunrise - and by Osiris of the night.

Maat, goddess of order and truth, make straight the god's path! Sekhmet the Powerful, lion goddess of Memphis - and The Great Illuminer: go forward, forward before the lord! And in the vessel the gods attend. The jackal-headed companion to Anubis: Opener of the Ways; and Sia, Hu and the Lady of the Barque who is the Maiden of the First Hour - and The Steersman too.

In the back the darkness persists and rock outcrops cast shadows. Eyes here are hidden - eyes of those who supplicate, those who hide their forms in fear of Flesh-of-Re's brilliance and those who lift their arms into the light, raise forearms and outstretched palms:

We have given offerings. We have listened, sung, chanted in evening light. We have kept free the feasts, measured fields with precision, filled jars of emmer to you, Oh Re. We have called out to you in the heat of the day.

The figures' cries:

Re, give sanctuary, preserve from the fires, from the serpents and guardians, from the night!

But the figure of Flesh-of-Re; the horned, slightly moving head of the ram - the was-sceptre in his hand - Flesh-of-Re, the standing figure, makes the slightest stir and the rays stab outward, they burn. In the recesses the bright light picks out bronze, wetted surfaces; picks out too, the cadaverous figures, hidden ones: the shapes behind pillars, figures in alcoves, the dust-covered, broken; the despairing.

Flesh-of-Re, enters the cavern. Amulets glint in these bright rays, the light shines through The Steersman and the other figures in the barque. There are no shadows at all. Dust on the mummiform figures, dust from the stars: emerald, ruby, amethyst, ultramarine, jade, diamond - glinting dust from between the stars, the remnants of dead stars - moments of anguish caught amid the bright glare between sun and moon. These momentary passages between night and day. There, life to be summed, the origin of the dream.

And such dreaming might contain each divided feature of lives by the river, lives embraced by the sun in the reed-bed river mouths and in moments of contemplation: the appearance in bright daylight of each dressed stone, each pyramidal slab, each dedication to be witnessed and each use of the tally-stick upon counting livestock and the days of all lives. Dance, dance the Muu: and the ba-souls of Pe might then be evoked - these, forms of the pharaohs of old – from before the dynasties, before all recollection; ba-souls of Pe, guardians of the king. They gather at each tombside, they hear the laments of all assembling; cries from recently dead men:

Oh God! Save, save, save Flesh-of-Re! The ripples spread outward, we move and each reflection carries recollections, the memories from dry dust and moments in silence - the dance of the waters.

Dance of rain in the desert. The greatest gift arising and the storms gathering. The god Min of fertility; to rise and be spoken of, whispered about, gestured towards, held in fear. The desert land and the

invisible figures standing - tall as the pillars at Waset,
at Giza the Pyramids, the unseen people of the desert,
the striding figures in this dry land; the visions
besetting a single pharaoh's nights - long dead: small
animal movements, unfamiliar fluid vibrations of
walls and linens. Tapestries blown in the desert wind,
the shadows behind pillars, the sounds, scents,
movements of a desert kingdom and the soldiers'
progress over deserted mountains: the land rises
before them, land of the new stars, the search for new
animals, plants, and for gazelles, hippopotami,
baboons, the giraffe and the bee. Crawling, singing,
the small movements in the night, a pharaoh's prickly
heat and ice, ice, ice and snow. We praise the snow
once carried by travellers here to a suffering lord.
New ice, cold, new stars unknown, new animals too,
heavens and an underworld await. These elements are
danced before the lord: Flesh-of-Re, transformed Re.
And those deficient in details, in spells, words, shabti-
figures, votive offerings, correct terms of address are
seen to falter. We dance on, we dance such
obeisances and move hands in upward flowing motion
to reverse, to offer up the trickle of water down
dressed stone surfaces; the passage of damp trails in
sand in the desert; the movement of scorpions,
beetles, the scarab of the dawn: waiting, the hope of
the Underworld; morning light, the sun-god's rise,
defeat of all fears.

This water, ocean, primordial chaos: the Nun circles
all and we know that this land of Egypt, this earth
surrounded in all directions, east, west, upward and

beneath our feet; and this undifferentiated sea: infinite, existing for all time containing all opposites, the eightfold writhing differences, the qualities - these primordial waters - can give rise to each separated consciousness, to the gods and these men who surround us; and to the rise of the Nile in the early year, the growth of corn and the clouds which pass in the winds above the desert.

Nun, father - the waters. Our arms and hands flicker, our arms sway; our bodies rise and fall with wave motions at the sides of boats drifting in the Nile. We gesture falling rain, seas in tempests, water pools collected between rocks and trapped there daily: the moisture drying as blood on open wounds from battles in Libya and Nubia, we gesture the sea-borne journey to the southern land, land of Punt.

We represent these enveloping waters. In each direction infinite - and we form the bubble cavity in this unending water; no upward surface and depths in each direction; in these waters the presence alone, god Atum, the progenitor - and the eightfold properties will writhe their presence too. They will move and join the reconciliation of all forces and the identity will stir and bring forth air and space, the land and sky. But a Mound will rise as these waters sink and the primordial river, our river, will be father to the Mound. Can this land rise swiftly, and in the heat and light, become dried - and give rise to all life? Can this be the origin of the fair land of the Nile? And this Nun, primordial water, can this then give rise to the two rivers: in the Underworld, the River of Urnes - and the origin of life in the two lands, the Nile?

But the writhing beings: the Darkness, Invisibility; the Inertness, Infinity; the Nothingness itself? In this way can we know the Nun - and the two rivers? These absences, darknesses, where no sound is heard and no light seen? Without direct vision will we meet them in the Underworld, the Duat - and Nothingness itself? Will these forms - faceless - meet us in the abyss? These primordial gods before the pharaohs themselves: in the dark by the greatest river, by the fires in the night. The figures without forms, the gestures which recall these shapeless waters: above, below, the waters to east and west.

We cannot see these gods and goddesses nor the first impulse: Amun and his Amaunet. What awaits us in the caverns, each serpent spitting fire, each decision to be made between life, death after death; the second death? Annihilation of these souls; broken, to nothing.

The abyss. Such absences, such vacuity - without the occasion for growth or the impulse even to change. The state like that before water freezes, the moment before spicules penetrate through the liquid body. A suspended moment, the state held there, poised, unnatured, the moment disallowed, the time before time of the universe itself?

And the cavity, ovum, this world to be broken, opened, to give rise to all light and hope; the future in expectation, the occasion of development, the new, the opening, the flowers and petals of the flowers, the lotus, lotus, lotus.

Blooming in the morning: the elevation, in the waters, rising to the light of the morning sun - and the fragrance, of Nefertum before the light on the small pool. Is this then the hope, this, then the future? Will these ideas first develop before the changes that embed themselves in matter: massive, the changes of the ice spicules stabbing across the infinite ocean? Each instant of thought has its origin in this single moment of the light on the water: light in the flower, odour for the lotus, the moment of morning.

Give rise, give rise. From nothing at all there will grow each property unknown, each essence later to become the very nature itself of figures in the world, figures in these worlds of the dead gods; gods able to awake only upon the passage of the bright sun in caverns. Rise gods: the dead ones, forms from before thought and before speech, presences in the dark caves, caves in the mountain tops, caves by the sea. Awake! Awake first to these signs of fertility, to the gentle movements of limbs. Oh gods, can we anticipate every hope in this future in the great land, land of the river, land of the Nile?

We hope and we breathe this air. Mountain air, this desert air, this air with the freshness of rain. The figure of Min will appear in this form and the derived gods too. Can we foresee these forms in the twilight, in the blaze of the sun and in cloud and in the night? Cold in the desert, rain on these rocky outcrops. The images emerge from hope, they console and beckon every fine day. Each gesture to produce the water dance itself - to indicate mother, father, the rise of the son from hope itself. And the son to act bravely, to meet dangers fearlessly.

The outcomes, the eventualities which we have never conceived and never might fear: the figures through which light passes, upright - steering the barque. In the prow protecting the sun-god: Sia, Hu, the figures in the nightly journey, and the sunlight burns through them and their slight transparencies pass over the rocks, move by the entrances and descend with the whirlpools into the caverns in the Duat, they pass with the god towards the region below.

We tremble. Tremble to approach the brilliance of the barque of the sun-god himself. Such fearful steps must never betray the small faults of lives spent: hopefully we demonstrate the acquisition of correct ancient forms; words spoken throughout a life in the hot sun.

We move nearer the shimmering barque, we will await the smallest gesture of acceptance by the sun-god; the advance towards the form which scintillates, the god of our loss. Speak now the spells, names of primordial forms. And there are forms without eyes;

without mouths, tongues - and forms without a head or face. Speak the name of the guardian snakes!

See, the serpent spits fire above the whirlpool in the River of Urnes - crying and wailing, figures supplicate then move!

The light dazzles and all features become drowned out. The approach to the sun-god: figures merge with each other and the planes, surfaces, curves and all notions of form and space become uniform, the blessed light. United: each bend and fissure and all inner structure too. Undifferentiated - such light - and the supplicants are indistinguishable too. Will they blend, become form like the god? Ocean water before the ice: water, the water dance and the passage on the River of Urnes.

Will the figures, united, pass through the darkness and into the dawn?

Chapter Nine

SUNSET

Cry of the suffering ka-souls, the sun-god abandons the unprepared ones, the accepted ba-souls travel with the Barque of Re.

A passageway leads down. The vision forms: the deity accepting the spoken phrases, garnering the ba-souls, moves towards the cavern. The gates swing open and the fire from the raised head of the serpent, Sia-Set, courses down in an arc. Light from the pool of fire flickers in the rock recesses before the brilliance of the god's light, the god's aureole; and the light penetrates this first entranceway.

The faces of the discarded, failed figures dull in the red glow and the sun sets. The mists which gather at night are reddened in the west and this light becomes reflected among bright surfaces on the earth. The light filtered by clouds passes among clay vessels and from reflecting surfaces; in tubes, tunnels, hollow spaces of all kinds: within water jars, in the vessels containing unctions, in the interiors of drinking jars hanging from the bronze projections in storehouses containing grain.

And red is the colour of light reflected through ruby necklaces and the garnets that catch at the light of the desert at sunset and whenever the dusty winds flow between unseen and moving forms. The crimson horizon is seen through them; each gesture then is picked out amid a greater transparency in the cloud of sand from the desert, dust from the western desert; the reddened detritus in the region where the disconsolate forms dwell. In the necropolis these translucencies gather; in the silences of their tombs the ka-souls gesture their despair, they repeat the movements and expressions of a lifetime; the way they ate and loved and worked - and covered great distances. These abandoned figures, visible only when the reddest of rays pass through them from a descending sun, these abandoned ones cry out; depart - they are caught sight of only occasionally when the crimson light is reflected from clouds. While their ba-souls attempt flight - and are defeated; while they mourn their lives - and are forgotten; these forms are noticeable only when the desert sand is seen through them; when the subtle changes become evident to the eye.

Then, oh then, can the traveller see the ka-souls' dance: the upraised arms and the gestures to their departed lord. For in this time between the day and the night, when the stars appear and drift westward, these figures too move towards this departing light - and their hands are wrung, their eyes are cast down and their dance - as of the waterfall, rainfall, the Nile flow, the moisture on the forehead of those in hard labour - this dance of the whirlpool grows of its own. The steaming water pool and the shining sun-god, form of all hope. These figures, partially seen, gesture all moments between the drip and fall; between the torrent and the flood.

In these moments, then *mention, mention of the departed lord.*

The dancers of this world of water indicate by raised arms the flight above their heads of night birds and of the passage of the river of the sky. The stars rise and set throughout the night and the dancers make their obeisance to the exempted stars of the north - those that circle the pole, paradise of their lords and pharaohs - those that are privileged, able to disdain; are unaffected indeed, by the water-borne passage of the sun-god through the Duat at night. And these Imperishable Stars that circle the pole but neither rise nor set; these stars able to avoid all passage through the Underworld, these stars are the reflections and resting places of the greatest forms still. We praise these skies.

Below, the red rays rise. From the desert in the west, figures in their water dance gesture amid drying rays on the desert sands. Can these ripples in the rays, ripples in the sands and ripples in the fall of water from the sky remain: portals in the Nun, primordial sea - and may the sand then be lapped by them? In the depths at the desert's edge can these figures bring out sweetness, the scarlet desert flowers and the rise of the lotus in the small silence of enclosed water?

Water, and the setting sun is seen through the small reflections on the surface. The recollection of each gesture and flowing movement - of the robes of favoured temple officials - and of the moments when flames too become extinguished: all such instants coalesce and become the very essence - the need, broken remains. And dew will settle on the wounds of soldiers slain in battle. (Blood sinks into the desert sand and the moisture meets rocks; is dried out and minerals become fractured. Each corpse then sinks beneath the sand.)

In that moment, invisible arms are raised to the sky and to the god of the sky, the sun-god, Re. Red rays of the image in the barque burn down. At this latest moment the god may be approached - and thus may a great crowd come near: of dead soldiers, dead scribes and women departed in childbirth, broken in disease. Pain, and the bright crimson moments when light is filtered through lids closed and suffering:

Such suffering now! We cry, cry, great god Re! To your departing presence - the death among red rays, of the image transforming. Your dead form now, Flesh-of-Re!

And thus the ram-headed god is preserved in the shrine, is protected by the serpent's coils, floats on the barque, is guided by The Steersman - in the company of Isis and Nephthys and of Sia in the prow - is hauled by four gods of the first hour of the Underworld; in this way departs the god from the sky.

The sun descends, the sun sets. Nomarchs and priests die, gather at the mountain, Manu, and all abandoned figures cry out amid reddened sands in the desert - and the solar barque floats on with the spirit-forms, with ba-souls of those never to be refused. The chosen, the creatures to become creatures of the night, the companions of Flesh-of-Re, the souls to be weighed, assessed by the Underworld judge, by the god of the rise of water in vegetation; sap in stems. The growth of papyrus on the river bank, the lotus in the enclosed pool.

Gentle light on the small and silent pool, the rosy-petalled lotus. The rise of Wenen-Nofer: Osiris, pharaoh, Judge of the Dead. Osiris, lord!

Vermilion. And the sands in the western desert disappear. The sun's departing rays, catching at exposed surfaces, remain red. The memory, too, of the Nile in flood, the lights in the cave entrances in highlands in Libya, in desert regions in the south, in the separated land: Punt. The sea moves smoothly by and there in the city the sight too of stars that are crimson; the reddened passage of the eclipsed moon, the flowering plants from highest altitudes, born of the snow, trapped by the snow and in this manner displaying rosy petals towards a dying sun. See, the god becomes ram-like! Dead, the Flesh-of-Re now in the Duat. The birds circling with downstroke wingstrokes display lower feathers in the dying glow; reflect to the earth below the fading colours of the decline of the sun. Red remains.

Scarlet between the grains of sand. Reflected and refracted. The rays display the origin of light in turbulent stars, in the spaces between the smallest particles and wherever one such creation passes near enough to its fellow: the universe in a point, singular, the many origins of the brightest worlds.

Into such swirling vortices may the vision be entrained, trapped in contemplation, and the sight of these sparkling points in time is the vision of Re, Flesh-of-Re. We search within these brilliants for The

Becoming, the morning, the rise in the eastern horizon, great god Khepri, scarab, the dawn.

The sun sets. Flesh-of-Re is gone. Alone in the night the departing forms return to familiar places. Unseen, they fade. Each indistinct gesture reflects the last failing attempt at coming forth into day. As the chill of the night proceeds, each movement of hand, eye and breath itself fades. Night and the vanishing; night and all recollection is gone. Night: the last unseen breath to be drawn. Stars climb from the eastern horizon towards the west. Night: and all spirits are gone.

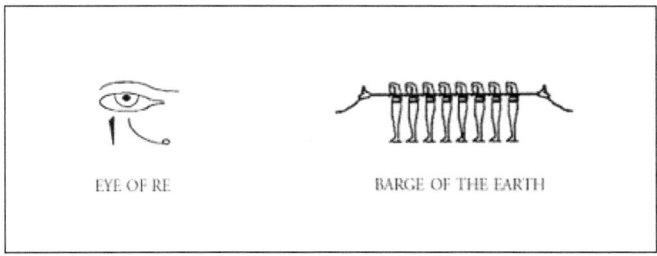

EYE OF RE　　　　　BARGE OF THE EARTH

Chapter Ten

THE TEARS OF RE

Re creates Shu and Tefnut, the Eye of Re weeps for its children. The Creation.

The night progresses. Above the land of the Nile, the stars rise in the east and ascend in the sky. Towards the north, the Imperishable Stars turn about the pole and never rise, never set. They avoid the Underworld; do not follow the sun-god and the others, the Unwearying Stars; do not descend to the mountain, Manu, the western horizon; do not enter the Duat.

The second hour - the country of Urnes. The gate protected by the raised and vertical serpent, Sia-Set, closes behind the Barque of Re. The Flesh-of-Re stands on board - protected by Mehen, serpent of the boat. The serpent's coils above the head of Flesh-of-Re cover the naos-canopy and honour the lord.

As this gate closes, as the light within the barque - from the dead sun-god himself - as this light becomes shut off abandoned souls cry out their loss and, weeping, fade into night.

The god's light reaches into the second cave. Where the river of Urnes flows between sand and where rocks outcrop to rise to the walls towering above, there the forms of devoted ones, The Praisers, have rested in silence, and all recollection of light and air is gone from their black eyes; and the glint of amulets, sceptres, head-dresses, badges of office is all that is seen. They are souls stilled from the life of air and light above. And the beautiful river of Hapi, the Nile, drifts slowly beyond the cataracts and slowly towards the delta; the reeds by the river flutter in breezes and the insects move amid reflections of the bright sky in waves.

With sudden awakening these spirits are stirred by the bright light - in the black cavern - of the sun-god himself. Singing arises, his praises are heard. For the great god will be united with the sons of Horus - Hapy, Imsety, Duamutef and Qebehsenuef - who rise with the lotus and here protect the viscera of the dead; who guard the cardinal points: the direction towards Manu and the western desert; and towards the eastern horizon of Khepri's rise, to Bakhu the mount of sunrise; to the northern delta and to the cataracts of the south.

And Osiris-as-the-moon precedes the barque and Isis-as-Hathor too. For Hathor was sent to avenge the sun-god in his old age and so brought about the death of men - of the Tears of Re.

Weep Re, weep for the loss of children, weep for the act which brought about creation in the Nun. And the Eye-of-Re-in-your-name-of-Atum: weep for rage at usurpation, at the loss of your divine place and of the Air and of Mist, the most insubstantial of children, lost; and the waters of Nun then might close.

In the Nun, primordial ocean: no direction preferred and these passive depths existing always. Nun: uncomprehending and the father of all. But the father of the gods, Re-in-your-name-of-Atum, stirred within the waters: turbulence, motion directed, desire and the origin of the idea. At first insubstantial the desire was able to create its simulacra: moisture, mist - and air. And the creator was to spit these out: children within the Nun. In the waters then, three gods. What was to follow was the dispersal of the darkness: the shapelessness; this infinity.

But the god Re-in-your-name-of-Atum was then to ascend upon a Mound emerging from the waters: the Mound which appeared - as islands in the Nile might be revealed after the flood. As the floods departed and the Nun departed the first germ, the cavity, appeared; the ovum of the kingdom of the two lands, Egypt, land of the Nile.

And the children wandered far over the water's surface, the air and the mist. Father, Re, alone once more. Weep, god Re-in-your-name-of-Atum. Abandoned, the single progenitor, active principle, the creator, singularity and the first movement of all.

In loss, in emptiness, in fear and in the remnant of hope, the god Re-in-your-name-of-Atum makes the Eye of Re depart, move across the waters of Nun far from the Mound, and The Eye travels in search of the children who have abandoned their father and returns with the two: Shu and Tefnut - Air and Mist - the brother and the sister with but a single soul.

And the Eye of Re saw that it was usurped and that the moon now shone above the dark water and anger arose in The Eye dispossessed.

The Eye suspended above the water, above the infinite ripples on the surface; vast in the shadow of the Mound and of the great god himself; in the moonbeams on the water, the moon itself shining. And Air and Mist envelop the sight and the anger of The Eye of Re is blotted out, concealed.

Weep, weep The Eye! For the son and daughter of the god; weep for the disposition, displacement - and the father's loss and The Eye's loss and all fear and broken love. In the first moment of this universe; in the dispersal – Air and Mist - and the tears formed overwhelming The Eye; and in the moonbeams bright tears fell.

Oh fragile light from the moon over the waters! What will become of tears shed into these unfathomable seas? Weep tears. Weep Re! Weep The Eye of the god of the Mound - and the drops descend. On the surface of all that might follow: on the Mound, the origin of our anguish and our hopes too.

The tears to become Man, tears to become *mankind*; the origin of all endeavour - and that which is human so forms in the tears.

At first within each droplet, the glint of an inner eye. The refracted light from the moon above the ocean of Nun is caught and reflected in each droplet as it falls, betraying the first flicker of emotion at the appearance, indistinct at first, of a sparkling, excited - a joyous gaze. Within every drop - these Tears of Re - the outline of Man; of men and women descending.

And the Mound extends to the horizon: the land to become peopled in this way. The descent of mankind from Re in the sky, and the divinities of Mist and Air, Tefnut and Shu, circle and witness the descent to the land below, land of the two kingdoms, of Hapi, the Nile. These deities circle: the cloud of tears, mankind itself, to fall like dew on every exposed feature of the landscape and there to embrace the land, love the land, to make home this land of the sun, Re, and of the River Nile.

Peopled. The rise of the kingdom of the two lands and of Libya, Nubia and Punt. And mankind spreading and living in caves and sheltering by the sea - in the mountains and deserts and by the Nile; in stranger lands to the south. Live Re-in-your-name-of-Atum!

Tears of Re, live!

Chapter Eleven

THE SACRED BARQUES

The procession of the barques. The ba-souls who suffer a second death, Flesh-of-Re is greeted by the Sons of Horus. Osiris.

The dead gods wait in the darkness in the second cavern of the Duat, wait fearful yet hoping for the appearance of the light of the sun-god - and the procession of the barques. For with this daily journeying of the god Re himself through the heavens - and with the transformation of Re into Atum and Atum into Flesh-of-Re; and the birth of each new day with Khepri, *The Becoming;* with all of this - and with the struggles nightly of the sun-god in the Duat - with the rise of the gods themselves in the desert; the gods viewed distantly over the seas and in lands with strange stars nightly circling overhead; with the cries of infants in reed-bed river mouths - with such struggles, such gods and strange stars - with the ba-souls of Pe and of Nekhen, the guardians of dead pharaohs from the lower and upper Nile; with all these mankind grew and mankind prospered: the children of the Tears of Re.

And the god's handiwork and the children of the god were seen in desert places. The animals whose strength, cunning and fleetness of foot might be desired - whose customs at dawn such as the worship of the rising sun - whose ability to live in the Nile waters - whose fierceness and whose flight in the clear air above the turns in the river - whose flight itself might soar to invisibility in deep blue skies; of necessity all such beings and beasts and birds of prey were at once the repository of the essence of the deities: each tree and flower and every ear of corn; all were animated in this divine way.

Beings: each moment, breath, each bending of an ear of corn - and the eyes of the gods looked out upon man.

And the crimes, too, and deceits and the blasphemies of man. There were temples abandoned, incantations neglected. There is gold - and there is silver measured out falsely and the small hatreds for the due observance of the worship of the lord.

The neglect of the devotion to the sun-god, Re. There have been Sumer and Ur; there is the divine knowledge of the men to the south. Within the kingdom of the two lands - and working evil - are the enemies of Re!

In the second cavern of the Duat, the spirits of these enemies are to meet their deaths a second time. However, within the kingdom of the two lands, their last breath had been heard; however their last words had come to be spoken; however, indeed, the collapse of their wills had come to occur; whatever the anger, relief or grief of those close when such blasphemers passed from light into darkness - into the Duat - there, there for ever would be the judgement; and in the Duat, the torment and the final execution. There would be the final suffering, final extinction; blackness beyond night, the end of the soul: oblivion and the death for a second time.

And the tormentors within: Benti; Iana-the-baboon-faced; Khnemu-of-the-two-corners and Sekhet-of-Waset - these wait for such souls. They wait to carry out the command of the lord of the sun in his solar barque who will illuminate the Duat and will pass through its caves.

The forms will scald and with knives torment; and these souls then are to be burned, burned as the vessel approaches! Weep, weep for this disregard - weep before the gods Neper-of-grain, Horus-of-the-two-faces and Makhy-of-the-sickle, who place these souls in the cavern at this hour, who bring destruction upon the blasphemers against Re!

In the country of Urnes the sun-god Re is to be greeted by the sons of Horus: Hapy, Imsety, Duamutef and Qebehsenuef. Their long tresses will flow to form pillars, pillars of iron; iron supports for the heaven above and the stars. Here they guard the cardinal points - which are the directions from which winds may blow - and each of the Sons of Horus arising from the lotus will protect the viscera of the blessed dead; will turn with the stars, the decans, which march with the night across the sky of Egypt above.

Feed, feed these gods and the lord Osiris, controller of this dead land, will gesture towards Re, will share out these lands and the wealth in this dark kingdom; and the light of Re in the cavern will awaken all within.

Iron, iron; the pillars, winds, viscera; rise of the lotus in the morning - Sons of Horus alive.

The Barque of Re is preceded by the four vessels of the Duat. By the first, Osiris-as-the-moon, and there at the head of the procession on the River of Urnes is the goddess Maat herself: order, correctness, truth; and the moon's light shines silver on Maat's head-dress of feathers. The ostrich feather - erect - of truth, justice; the balance and order of all. Nothing is to upset the passage of the sun-god, no disturbing influence and the face of the beautiful moon is to be the guiding influence: Osiris, god of the dead and shining now in the crystalline light of the moon itself.

The second vessel - Isis-as-Hathor - and the sistrum sounds and the echo returns from the cave walls and all crevices; from the nests of serpents, coiled, curling away from the light, from the sun-god's rays. The enemies of Re will shrink from the sound; be confounded by these echoes and their cries, echoing too, will cross and interweave:

All is lost, lost, all is lost!

But for the faithful to Re, in this barque is the emblem of the future in silence: Khepri, *The Becoming,* the scarab; not yet the dawn.

Yet further behind: the vessel of Anubis and Wepwawet, of the summer solstice and the winter - The Embalmer of the Dead and The Opener of the Ways; their jackal heads moving in time with the rocking of the boat over rapids. Aboard the vessel, the crocodile, larger than any man, lies with back split wide open and the head of a man penetrating. The fissure: the head protruding from the reptile's spine; the neck penetrating through the scaly hide and the eyes of the man looking forward, forward to the prow with the white crown of the southern kingdom - and behind the beast, too, the red crown of the north.

116

The human head looking forward, the vessel of Anubis and Wepwawet preceding the solar barque: in this way every turn in the river of Urnes is made certain. And with care - causing the crocodile tail to move only slightly; causing the back to be stilled and no tremors then to enter the water from the boat's wooden sides - in this manner the ways of the lord are to be made open.

No ripples now, the water stilled for the approach of the Barque of Re and of the barque's precursor - of Osiris-in-your-name-of-Grain. This itself is scorched by the brilliance of what is to follow. There are women without arms who accompany the god - Osiris - of vegetation, of grain and the rise of seedlings in a hot sun. God of fertile growth in waters shallow and warmed by a cloudless sun; god of green growth above; of food; plenty; the wealth of the Nile.

For Osiris is king of the Duat, of the dead of this land, and makes safe the path for the god of the sun, for Flesh-of-Re himself. In this dead form, the sun will illuminate the territory of the dear one - Osiris, the father of Horus, the dismembered one of the night. The kite-bird of Isis, wife and sister, will rise above the corpse and there at once: *light* - and the fathering of the god-pharaoh, of the Horus-god himself. Osiris alive in his member; Osiris, dismembered throughout the land. Thirteen-fold burial and the god Seth rages, seeks fourteen-fold from the cataracts to the delta. Seth so seeks the twisted remains and Seth, of the hippopotamus, will fight with Horus, Osiris' son.

Horus: Isis' offspring and son of the lord of the djed-column. And Seth will rage before the Ennead of the nine gods: Seth to be condemned in judgement; Seth, of

117

the fearsome deed. Osiris now in the Duat, ruler and god. Praise lord, protector of Re, Osiris, judge over all!

We will enter before Osiris in the Hall of Judgement - the heart weighing against the Feather of Truth - and there Maat of the upper kingdom and Maat of the lower kingdom will inform the forty-two assessor gods. Thoth will judge the balance when equal, Anubis observe these elements and Thoth will record the facts of all lives.

Silence, in the dark; far from the pharaoh and alone in the reed-bed channels, far from comfort and the relief of torments at night, the banishment of visions - the release of all hopes that rise above the earth: the constraints no more. Hopes from the vision of redness in the morning, from the dew trapped among grasses; and all might shiver with hope, wait for the sun of full day and recall only moments from the night.

We see before us the golden light on the horizon; we see where dust and fragrance rise from the land, the peaks of distant lands.

Such moments are brought about by chance - the fracture of a frozen rock in bright sunlight, the collision on mountain tops of rocks by cave entrances. Each feature is to be noticed by a more acute vision which penetrates even mists on the summits. All further expectation would be certain to be fulfilled. Each contact made by mists with mountain peaks would cause light and dark to alter; the passage of sunlight over rocks to be cut off and then to shine out suddenly: and this would be seen by certain figures in groves of thick vegetation; and by men far distant on boats out at sea.

Across this burning land hopes might then be communicated and the awareness of whispers then form suddenly:

Now, and now, this surely - and this, this too! This now is mention of the lord!

Chapter Twelve

APOPIS

The shrines of the silent gods, the eight primordial deities and the darkness of the abyss, Apopis attacks the Barque of Re.

The sun-god passes from the second hour of the Duat. Now that he has been adored by these beings; now that he has passed by these deities; now that Re's light has spread to the furthest recesses of the cave; now that dead spirits have been revived, have called out for sustenance; now that the sun-god has measured out their gifts; now that the direction forward has been indicated; now that the second hour is thus complete and the river flows on, flows towards the cavern gate; now all this has taken place, still more caves begin to appear: deeper - deeper, and more fearsome still the beings which are to come, more terrible, too, the echo of their cries.

And the gates of the third hour are protected by the guardian, Qaby-the-coiled-serpent. These gates are set into the rock itself - and beyond there is a corridor, and fires descend from serpents' mouths. A sharp indrawing of breath.

The rock upon which Qaby coils - upon which, protected by water, Qaby rises higher; upon which Qaby ascends to the roof of the cavern, there to be assuaged only by the company of gods - of Re himself - this rock is soon to be overwhelmed by the water of the river of Urnes. Qaby then is to be seen rising above all heads - higher than the naos-canopy on the Barque of Re – and into the vault itself. For at the cavern's highest point, the head of the serpent uncoils to spit fire at figures moving below. And the fire tumbles down - and the body of the raised serpent undulates with each breath.

From the Barque of Re the title: Sharp-of-flame, is heard, it rings out before the entrance so that the gates themselves might be named.

Above the river, the gates swing slowly open and the vessels slip forward. The blessed Flesh-of-Re moves towards the third cavern of the journey of the dead form of the god - the journey through the Duat and before the dawn.

The torrent through the gate sweeps the Barque of Flesh-of-Re into the cavern of the third hour. Echoing from every rock wall and every prominence then come the cries of the dead ones, the poor spirits. From among the temples of gods in rocky recesses; in alcoves high above the river; in valleys overhanging the river and on the cliffs. Cries come from within these shuttered and closed shrines. And a stirring and the first flicker of a light is to be seen; the final movement of the doors opening and the clear sight then of the divinities themselves picked out in the small light from votive lamps: mummiform, illuminated from below by the disk of the sun-god himself.

These deities are imprisoned, trapped by their protector. In the dim light, this form is hardly visible at all. A shadow perhaps over one of the shrines: a loop between another two on opposite sides of a valley into which no light at all has ever penetrated - the dark hills under the cavern roof - land of no daylight, no rain, no winds at all. And no growth except the silent accumulation of minerals by water, the development of rocky projections deposited from the overhanging cavern roof; a world unseen, silent. In the distance water drips.

What suffering is this? What deeds forgotten, what memories of the pious in the land? What love lies dying, what gentle memories?

There are children among the reeds. What reflections are there in the sunlight as the Nile barge of the pharaoh slips silently by; what recollections of a life in the sun and happiness?

Do these memories return in the dark? Loss; will there be any memory persisting: recollection, re-union, any moment caught unknowingly after the momentary closing of the eye? A flicker and a remembrance of a moment of happiness, of the wine made sacred and the barley cakes eaten devotedly too - of shadows stabbing outward from the sun temple and of the shade of the pylons at Waset - here a votive offering, a deity beyond the temple, an altar on the outer wall. Reed baskets carry offerings, and the ducks and geese move without noise and the ibises rise in flight and the wind blows husks of corn far off. Far, the air rises; seeds spiral in flight.

Bread, emmer beer, the family sits alone and the lights go out singly. The child sleeps and one by one the lights vanish in lines: making the paths, causeways and areas of danger vanish. The lights are suspended in the wind at night and now - all danger spent - the water laps at the side of the boat: water drips and oars turn in the waves.

In the dark third hour, in the third cavern of the Duat - each recollection is a sparkling point of light in the darkness, the black of an unknown space. Each point then is to be approached, observed - the world in a sunlit moment; in an embrace. These preserved, undying; no longer connected and now separated by the blackness - such fragments persist alone in the dead minds: flickering moments of lives long spent.

And a deeper darkness exists, its remnants coil in wait in this space. In the continuing moments before Re-in-his-name-of-Atum formed in the waters, a shadow once surrounded all: there was foulness and an infinite blackness. In this space now, for the sun-god himself - the greatest threat.

Return to that emptiness and the eightfold forms: to the chaos of the primordial abyss, the infinity; return to the darkness and the hidden power; power of the god Nun and the goddess Naunet, of Heh and Hauhet, Kek and Kauket, Amun and Amaunet - frog-headed and snake-headed these gods and goddesses, these writhing forms might displace Re-in-his-name-of-Atum. In each fissure where these elements might exist, in the spaces between rocks colliding on mountain tops; in the small cavities between water surfaces in flecks of foam; in the moment before the jar might crack in heat - and between the raising of eddies in sand. In the moments before such eddies might whirl high above the land - and in the minds of men.

And every sand particle is separated in this way. In the moments before moisture fills these spaces completely, before it turns the grains around by the force in water surfaces alone, in these moments jagged points will then catch at the air, sparkle in the small light and disturb all sunlight. There, amid crystal points of light in the Nile: there - there is darkness and chaos; the abyss.

Can each moment be like this? Is each moment separated by inner darknesses, are the eightfold gods present throughout every fibre; the gods in every echo, in each moment of this kingdom of the two lands, kingdom of the Nile?

And memory which threads between these isolated moments, which causes the approach and assimilation of the fairest days; flashes of bright light - this memory persists.

There are dead bodies, dead minds. A single vibration: a fragile association of each bright possession; each turn of the thread, fold of cloth and glint of beaten metal.

All may be thus preserved: the solitary ambitions, the love and excitement of the moments which shine singly; particular angles of each crystal face - the critical angles where light might sparkle and unite in direction - and memory might in this way re-form.

This arrangement to become the complex structure of discrete recollections: this interplay, remembrances abutting each other; in tension between each other and passing on among themselves one mode of vibration and another rate of rotation; the inversion, too, of one sequence of events, or of another arrangement of importance; of affection, perhaps even of fear.

All hopes and fear associated in this way; closely adjusted, vibrantly alive so that they are impelled to spin onwards forever, their special motions coupled to all around; to others persisting beyond life, beyond decay, beyond the final beat, final breath, the gesture of final laughter.

The light from the Barque of Re penetrates each shrine in turn, the débris of centuries within is disturbed as doors swing wide open and the dust - which at times rises to cover all but the heads of the mummiform deities within - this dust piled high, tumbles outward, slips down the rock face between cracks and in cloudy pools falls to the river below. Bronze and gold offering vessels, faience scarabs and the golden writing on each cartonnage reflect the rays of light back towards the solar barque. These light beams then make glowing stabs towards other rock faces, towards the river water in pools, and they catch at figures moving in the shades between rock pillars and at scaly beings too distant to be identified, too fearsome to be seen. And the river flows on amid these gesturing figures in the night.

Sia reveals the recollections of the deities in their shrines; their life's brief return while the sun's rays fall on them momentarily, sparkle briefly: a host of sun-filled memories and they then die in the shadows - in the return of darkness as Re moves on. They cry out at the loss of sustenance, the return of night's fears and the loss of all warmth, of the sun-god, Re.

But a greater force is impossible to constrain and light might thus become swallowed up in its containment even in the primordial waters. Re-in-your-name-of-Atum, creator in the infinite ocean; there, in the Nun, one other presence at that time persisted - the presence from before the universe of light: there, the swallower of the sun's rays, the greatest threat to the heat and light.

Dark sun, consumer of the light; the writhing presence, writhing threat; hatred, the fearsome form which moves in the water, roars; and the cavern reverberates and these echoes come from the other caves too. Each then sounds through gates in the darkness to come - and there are reverberations at every solid surface and in each hour of the Duat.

In this way, the creature in the darkness knows by such reflected sounds every rock and fissure, every rapid in the river of the Duat.

Fear, and the dark form opens its flinty mouth wide. Fear, and it devours even its own cries: the roars that shake each cavern gate.

For this is the form of no form at all; of the random and chaotic urges towards destruction, each black and hopeless moment, each darkness and loss of hope. The cry, cry of the loss of the sun in the river: death in the reed beds, all betrayed hopes and final disillusionment; the pain ending in death; the knowledge of all disasters, the suffering; the sudden indrawn breath at night, and the last gasps of animals dying in harnesses, warriors dying of wounds.

All hope gone! The writhing form approaches the Barque of Re; breathing in the echoes of its roars - echoes detailing the smallest features of all rock interstices; all moving beings; the twists of fleshy wings in winds in darkness. Above, in the kingdom of the two lands, the first portion of the sun itself might now be invaded, and the disk reduced while unnatural night descends. Diminished, eclipsed, and the conquering dark sun could envelop the whole.

Night, blackness and chaos, and in poisonous waters it might be possible to drift. Dark, turgid grip. Viscous fluids would then enclose unsympathetically the form possessed; enter vacuoles and body enclosures; work there against the will; assume all forms inimical to desires; cause decay, the acidic decomposition of the cavities in the heart itself; move simultaneously to the eyes - and burn inside. The head would expand within and be crushed without; in the torso strange movements indeed of alien forms disturbing body remnants: no rest for this departing soul. The darkness and the second death.

This form seen only now in the water - and curling through the cavern gate itself: thrashing, raising the flint head nearer by the moment; capable of bringing destruction even to the solar lord!

Will this then be the defeat of day? For the dark to prosper, only the derangement is necessary of what is now held dear; only the change in structure of desires and hopes - thus the darkness will remain to absorb all residues.

The disarray of desires, the disorder: night for day, and the decay from within at the fiery breath; the devouring of echoes. The darkness itself might then enfold the solar lord, might twist and turn about the bright form of the sun and obscure the light in its fleshy folds.

As each coil envelops the Barque of Re, the shadows of the form of evil writhe: of Apopis of the Underworld; Apopis, the darkness surrounding Nun - pre-existing and the nemesis of Re. These shadows of the serpent,

127

contorted in form, fall on the rock walls in the cave of the third hour, the third hour of the journey of Flesh-of-Re in the Duat.

Each thrashing movement is then projected grotesquely: a shadow on the shrines of the silent gods, on the closed doors, and on the figures which disappear quietly from sight. The water boils in the violent movement of head and tail.

The naos-canopy rocks and Apopis whose tail penetrates to the next gate of the Duat and whose head is raised, whose mouth is wide open above the vessel; Apopis, the serpent, springs his fangs wide and flames jet forth. Steam rises from the river of the Duat and the figures of the gods on board the vessel are rocked. No outcome is certain now that once more the form of darkness surrounds the figure of the creator-god.

The maiden of the third hour of the Duat and the figure of Sia gesture sudden movements as the head and fiery breath of Apopis descend to the Barque of Re and threaten their lord. The scales by the serpent's mouth are singed in the god's rays and The Steersman pushes the vessel till it spins out of the path of any lunge that Apopis might make; steers the barque quickly, and the gods of the third hour haul on the tow rope so that the vessel moves rapidly now towards the form in the distance of the open-mouthed head of the bull: the Barge of the Earth.

Apopis, with a writhing which begins at the flinty head and undulates along the scaled body to the coils surrounding the Barque of Re - this darkness, Apopis, follows the vessel and the figure of the open-mouthed bull-head looms nearer: the Barge of the Earth.

128

The gods of the hour pull towards the bull's head, they pull towards a huge column held level by half-seen deities in the dim light: the bull's spine. On the spine's upper surface, yet more indistinct forms emerge. Greatly distant, the far end of the Barge of the Earth is obscured by the night.

The mouth of the bull now hides the rock headlands above the River of the Duat, the torrents from caves at the foot of cliffs; hides too the enveloping form: the principle of darkness and the fear of all gods accompanying Re - of Sia and the Steersman and the Maiden of the Hour.

Make speed! Hasten toward the safe form opening before the Barque of Re, guide the solar lord! Direct and assist to the Barge of the Earth. In there the safety of the deep recesses, in there the obscurity of the underworld of the primordial ones: dreams of the silent ones, the unknown ones, lost ones; the dreams of those before speech; darkness, dark and unfamiliar forms; kings before the pharaohs. The territory which rises before the eyes unbidden in sleep; the foetid land before the two kingdoms; of tangled growth where now the desert of the west is seen. Of the cries of southern birds in damp branches; rain, rain in the day, the moist leaves and the vapour rising above the forest. The Nile obscured.

The river floods. The waters spread throughout the forest and the myriad insect forms disperse on the waters: a glistening sea and the hot sun burns through to raise vapours and burn the upper surfaces of those creatures exposed. The figures of men move between branches in the trees, float on broken trees. The water buffalo retreat to the farthest recesses and the territory of the Nile is an obscured land of forest insects, cries of night birds and the wriggling motions of silent acts of digestion; of parasitic worms.

These residues and the recollection of the world before the record - in stone and all memories chronicled. These visions flicker between the first indications; between the image and the symbol, the echo ricocheting among trees; among moss-covered rock outcrops in forest clearings. Bird cries, riotous growth trapped in the sands of the Nile overflowing.

Through each successive dream: this world and the dreams forming themselves from brackish water; from deep within the boles of trees, from ferns. The origin of language, intentions expressed forcefully - and the nearness of whispers.

Whispered then - the name of the lord amid a strange accumulation around forest pools. In clearings the water is stilled. The lotus rises from the bottom, the red rays of dawn and the petals open wide: essence, perfume of Nefertum. And the primordial presence flutters past, is glimpsed in undergrowth, becomes the essence of the dream; it will then form legends.

What truth persists? The glimpse through mists, as the ages pass; the forest's decline, the origin and the descent in the west? Can these whispers, strange eyes, and the word be known? Knowledge of primordial forms - and upright animals seek out the two horizons and in divine procession float free above the earth.

Chapter Thirteen

THE BARGE OF THE EARTH

Flesh-of-Re takes refuge in an underworld within the Duat. The Lake of Fire.

The roars of Apopis come nearer still, the figures in the Barque of Re cower nearer to the naos-canopy, blinded by the god's light. The tow rope pulls hard and the vessel slips within the bull's head, over teeth, the tongue, into the throat and the light from inside the naos-canopy reveals the first sight within the Barge of the Earth, of the vegetation and the leaf-formed figures within.

Apopis, breathing hard, writhes before the Barge of the Earth and the pursuit of Flesh-of-Re is lost. Apopis' coils sink below the water; currents swirl over scales of flint. Within the Barge of the Earth where none may follow there are no eyes at all to see the wonders, dangers and trials within. Only the hint seen through the bull's open jaws: the rich growth of an earlier Egypt, and Flesh-of-Re then passes from the Duat to that deeper world - earlier still and the remnant of the first land of the Nile.

Within, safe from the attack of Apopis, in darkness but subject instead to the strangeness of a world before the two lands, before recorded time: strange, the life of forests and daily rainfall.

The solar lord's dream. The dream to become first a part of all trees, leaves, raindrops and rivulets. Streams and the sun-god's rays falling on the droplets sparkle and turn: in all such reflections elements of the dream will arise. The passage through abandoned ways, through past forests: and in this dream of the sun-god what depth and what warmth?

Warm seas, circling currents, embrace of the Nun. Moments and aeons of time dispersed. In these secret ages and in formlessness: without direction; timelessness, no stirring at all but the enmity of darkness surrounding the Nun. The light lying within.

The instability of fluids mixing: oils and water, the generation of cavities within liquids. Air surfaces within the liquid mass. Coalescence and the formation of whirlpool currents, the conflict therefore of heat and the dark: the stirrings of familiar desires.

And the dream was to have so gradual a source. There might then be only a slight imbalance of inner light and darkness outside: at first, the images of swirling vortices - nearness and distance - and the passage of endless time, of isolated visions within.

The light of Re becomes cut off, the Barque of Re now moving within the Barge of the Earth: unseen in the primordial forest, the underworld of this Underworld; memory alone of these first forms. Primordial deities existing before recollection and all records; existing among the trees: ba-souls of Pe, ba-souls of Nekhen, guardians of kings. Above the Barge of the Earth may be seen the distinct forms of these gods themselves: gods lost in time; seven-fold division of the underworld of the Duat.

The gods above the Barge of the Earth. The appearance along the length of the Barge of these dimly seen figures: rulers' heads, other kings seated; unknown gods with unfamiliar features; the primitive forms, forest lords; the images from within, the solar lord's dream. The visions then of his journey through gates and the forest openings in an underworld unknown.

Will Flesh-of-Re emerge, ever to sail downstream as lord of the two lands, the father of Shu and Tefnut, begetter of all mankind?

These lords of loss cry out with all the suffering of the coldest dark nights. Without stars; fears in the darkness and the drop, drop of blood draining away; the fearful, dark, second death, the annihilation. All dreaming spent.

Cries come from the distance from the far side of the river; from the red and sulphurous glow of the Lake of Fire: the figures there caught occasionally behind clouds of vapour from the swirling surface - the figures which are half plunged into the boiling liquid.

The Lake of Fire behind swaying cornfields - here the souls, immersed but not yet burning, are preserved in terror. Untouched as yet, not able even to perceive their own fate; stilled, once silent observers - driven by hope perhaps; scorched, unmoving.

Stay, lord of the sun, stay!

The now burning figures in the Lake of Fire manage finally to exclaim, but the Barque of Flesh-of-Re will sail from the Barge of the Earth. Flesh-of-Re will emerge to pass directly now to the fourth hour of the Duat.

Chapter Fourteen

THE DEVOURERS OF THE HOURS

The nest of serpents, Sehereret and the birth of the Devourers of-the-hours, Great-of-dignity saves the Barque in the fourth hour.

Sekhemus: fourth hour of the night. The Barque of Re, entering from the Barge of the Earth, passes the raised and vertical serpent, Djedeby-the-slayer and the gate of the fourth hour: Mistress-of-offering; and passes the mummiform gods, Nuerbesta and Shaker-of-the-earth. Silent, these guardians - immobile - are able to deny access by their command of the uraei whose mouths - wide-open - throw fire in arcs down the corridor between the caverns. The flames curl round the corners, scorch everything that once might have been able to live and the waters of the river rise in steam. The roar of this fiery breath and Nuerbesta and Shaker-of-the-earth give way to their lord: almost no movement at all, but the uraei coil, slide between stones; at last disappear. Flesh-of-Re moves into the open space of the fourth hour.

Hours of the Night: guardians of each hour. The Maidens of the Hours gather around the nest of Sehereret. Coiled, the serpent writhes and gives birth to young: the Devourers-of-the-hours, and these maidens wait looking anxiously among themselves - each serpent birth to produce a devourer for that hour. The spirits in the Barque of Re know the protection that is necessary; the guidance, pilotage, words of control and advice: to each moment its dangers; to each hour its gentle assistance.

At the live birth, the cries of the Maidens of the Hours rise up, they venture then, glide hands through Sehereret's coils, grapple at each hour for the serpent birth: each maiden then and the new-born devourer. Death and the sliding, hissing, screaming, constricting, devouring, gorging; the strangling and the slicing of teeth on smooth scales; each Maiden of the Hour to kill or be killed - and the birth of each serpent now the greatest danger that the maidens: the Daughter-of-Mut, the Raiser and the Goddess-of-Sickness are ever to know. The writhing births - and the maidens must grapple and catch the new-born serpent by the throat, raise the snakehead to the mouth, bite hard into the serpent's scales, break apart each of its bones. The blood then will run down the faces of the beautiful maidens:

Great-of-dignity of the fourth hour, tell us, what must be done within!

But the goddess of the fourth hour of the Duat saves all within the Barque of Re: biting, tearing at the serpent's offspring, preserving this passage for the god of the sun. For the serpent birth is cut short and all maidens then break and twist the fourth-born serpent's spine, they tear the flesh to be eaten by Great-of-dignity, maiden of the fourth hour. So great a service to the solar lord! No

136

remnant then of this danger to the passage of Re through the hours of the night.

And the river of the Duat is here to be dried up: passing through narrow rocky confines, it drains into swallow-holes first in a whirlpool, then slowly it sinks into lower caves. The dark waters spread out onto the sands of a beach and the waves lap onto it: each ripple from the Barque of Re laps at the beach as it enters this cavern - at its greatest extremity it expends itself on a distant sandbar. And the company of gods and symbols - the ba-souls of thousands who fly about their lord - these move in and out of his light, cause shadows on the opposite cavern walls and the god is left to mark the beach alone: the singular traveller through the Duat; to penetrate further - to the land of Seker, lord on his sand.

Chapter Fifteen

SEKER

The river drains away, despair of Osiris, origin of Seker.

Seker, lord of the mysterious region, He-who-is-on-his-sand; great god of the winged serpent; divine one who came into being before the Duat who rests upon darkness; god of the Hennu boat:

Cry, cry the god!

In silence in the Duat, with the winds circling the caverns. Small movements of sand, sliding paces of beasts not seen but moving on their bellies, concealed in darkness, hidden amid the last of the disappearing water. The river - now vanished into caves - leaves in the end only damp spots in the burning, dry heat of the sand.

Sand and the cry alone, rarely to be heard, the moment of night. Cry of all the deaths and all the final agonies. Despair: the moment of the death of kings, the abandonment, all garments rent; no help, succour, all sustenance gone and the eternal vigil - alone - the eternal emptiness. All images now lost - and the cry alone which might of itself break a man's heart makes the birds of the air and the beasts of the earth to weep, weep against their nature: weep the loss of life, hope, of the love of brother, sister and wife.

Oh, help quickly! Hurry to me, sister, wife!

The scream of Osiris constrained, held in darkness; and death, death to Osiris, lord!

The cry alone preserved and echoing then in caves in the Duat. The shriek to take up *form*. The hawk-headed form, resting beneath the earth itself, the lord of this mysterious region, the cry to become Seker, lord who is upon his sand - cry of despair. Despair sustained, despair in the Hennu boat. Seker, lord, of Osiris' last cry. The scream preserved.

And the terror of the primordial Osiris, fear of the divine soul, blackness in the akh - illuminating principle - death of light unimagined, the collapse of the soul within; all desire to be lost, and the knowledge then of the abyssal depths. As each fragment of such special matter falls inwards among its fellows, the light itself is constrained; unable then to emerge, able only to make contact with other collapsed, fragmentary portions: the soul in death, extinction. A vain, too rapid vibration. The god no more.

Save and protect the great god Flesh-of-Re, in your quietness: these gods and helpers to protect the sun-god. All other sounds and cries will echo through the caverns and between rock faces. To cry then, Seker on his sand, and the great god Re will rise and illuminate the kingdom of the two lands. The Nile, this lord, the vision's vision. Never then to be disturbed, to be threatened, fractured; the vision preserved. What remains is sacred, whole: the dear form, dear life, the greatest protector - and the ba-souls from the land of Egypt might then pass with the great illuminator in safety through the Duat to Khepri's rise, to the horizon; to the Field of Reeds.

Will Seker, despairing cry of Osiris, break the will of the lord of the sun in the sky? At the echo of the cry, the currents of air from the wings beneath Seker will be felt; there then could only follow the passage through dark corridors of this remnant of the lord's despair; of the exhaustion of the air, of the dark closing of the coffin lid.

The cry has echoed through these corridors of the Duat in centuries and all illuminated forms: all petals and the irises of eyes, the rainbow in the desert after rain; the smallest ripples on water itself fade at the sound of the god's fear.

The ba-souls of the travellers with Re become alarmed and fly to the cavern roof, above the single form, bright in the empty space, the ba-souls move sudden wingstrokes and circle above the figure: their paths in the air to collect at certain points and to disperse elsewhere. In the cavern then the whisper of the cry of the dying god - and the sound itself, each sibilance absorbed and nullified by their feathered wings. Between nodes: the absorption of the dread sound; the fear beyond all imagining - and each traveller with Re then to arise and share that which is undreamed.

The nature of the sound itself may be read in the regions of the ba-souls' dispersal: the lines of arousal in the cavern air, the many polarities of sound. A fear to be seen as well as heard, to surround and to penetrate, to paralyse all.

No! Save, save the lord! The light too precious: so desired the night-time visitation of the suffering. No - for the passage of the sun in the day is to be preserved! For all hopes reside in the lord of the two lands. And Seker is known in the regions as darkness from before the records of time, primordial: the dark deity.

Save from the despair that curled once through forests, slid along sandy river beds and burned in the sun. All hope lost as the moisture dried from leaves, the foliage shrivelled - and then the silent fall of dry husks to the ground.

Save from the extinction of the will that might cause the final heartbeat: death of the unborn child, the dying remnants of a life before life. Each animal form that aspires towards divinity senses then the lowered eyelids, the heads which turn only further away. Despair and the broken columns no longer reach to the twist and turns of clouds in the sky, they are able to shut off no more light in the heat of noon. The face of all sons turns silently in death in the river.

The echoes and the sun-god falters. May a passage forward be uncovered? The dry land; dark, the sand burning in the night. Fearful beasts roam the regions of the land.

Seker in your underworld. Separate, the remnant - as in the Barge of the Earth - of a previous darkness. Before the forests dried, there was certainty to meet this dark lord; sure it was that within the Duat his underworld would be preserved. To proceed into passages and avoid each distinct sound - whenever the air moved in reverberation: there, the residue of the cry of Osiris, lord! The sound preserved, echoing from the single moment;

141

echoing through ages along passages and between rock faces, through the narrow confines and gates of the Duat. Oh world of such terrors, this Underworld! Give way, give way to light and the clear air above!

But in the passage of this lower world will be the renewal of life forms, the growth from his dead form of Re himself. What will be possible now, in the dark regions once denied?

On the perimeter of this land of Seker the guardians patrol: there is Menmenu-the-wanderer, with his seventeen heads, there is the great scorpion, Ankhet-the-living-goddess, and the three-headed Neheb-kau, yoker of souls. These make their journey daily - and the perimeter of the land of The-god-who-is-upon-his-sand is swept clear by their dragging tails. Live flesh and carrion are consumed by them on the spot.

All that falls to such beasts is crushed in massive jaws: blood is drained, flesh devoured; these guardians keep clear all approaches to the land of their despairing lord.

But Thoth accompanying the great god Re; Thoth of wisdom, of knowledge of the paths of Rosetjau; of the word written and discerned, Thoth will save and protect the sun-god Re, save and render him service. For in the dark, where giant boulders rise from the sand, there, cut into these rocks themselves the black entrance to passageways may be seen; and the doors to these passageways remain firmly shut.

Will brilliance, heat and light, meet and mingle with the dark? What figures, swirling images, turning points and collapses and expansions might there be then?

Can the images themselves take over their movements, dances, the paths in circles, the ellipses and curves returning infinitely to straight lines? What will the outcome of any such confrontation be? Can any such risks be contemplated, perplexities examined or dangers contained?

Will there be forms able to meet on such dazzling horizons? Horizons, and the hoped-for rise of the sun. The Becoming, birth, Khepri, the bright disc of Khepri, the scarab on the horizon at dawn? Can there be hope now for the sun to rise, in the journey through the Duat - a moment for hope to begin?

To preserve, hold separate, to save. The light of the sun-god burns. Rock scorches hard - the broken face of the hardest surfaces. Here at the entranceway, the legends of a thousand nights and millions of days; years, the passage of dynasties, the changes from the forest - all these to pass away; and in the return of the god, others make plain the intent, give account of this present passage - and of the last. The necessity to hope for the god's arousal - for this god now must be rendered distinct: Osiris, the lord. Sleep, sleep, dismembered sleep of the dead god, and the lord Re moves without the darkness. Despair. Can you, Osiris, have suffered so much? With your cry: the depths of the betrayal. What realisation is this? The great god and the god of resurrection too?

These followers, helpers, praisers - all are devoted to you, oh Re! To Osiris, lord in your pain. Such sufferers make the way clear for the god of the sun and soothe the cry in the night.

Chapter Sixteen

THOTH

The three doors and their passageways, Amemet the Devourer of Souls, separation of Seker and Re.

Nowhere, nowhere now. The inscriptions on the rock by the entrance mark Thoth's return. Thoth of wisdom - the god able to record and detail the minute changes in the hopes of men. All then recorded by the entranceway - and the deeds, desires, allegiances; the commands of the lord; the lusts, reveries and the intentions of the divine will set out. And Thoth was able to indicate every point of confirmation by motioning towards parallel wishes inscribed in stone; to every complementary command; to expressions of the love of form and wills brought forth together; to the close association of the Ennead of the nine gods; to the growth in the waters, and the rise in the morning of the light of the morning, of the lotus from the depths.

All conflicts to be discharged, all desires to be served, all despair preserved. Thoth, calling into the darkness to the echoing cry of Osiris lord, to Seker-on-his-sand, cries out for the god's despair unassuaged; the despair made complete. The whole structure interconnects: the criss-crossing echoes in the web of dark channels; air which is

144

forced down passages, the echo, never dying, of the lord's dark night.

Preserve this essence and the solar lord's brilliance. The sun's rays undiminished, the one to swirl about the other, to rise up unseen, to pass through channels unseen.

And the word is the deed. This Duat of imaginings, of endings and of destinies, of the summation of fears, of the exact balancing of reveries; this Duat is formed to meet all the divine needs.

How else might such a journey of the god, journey in night-time come about? The daily ritual of the sun's journey through the bright sky above - all sanctities to be preserved? The work of the god Thoth would then be to detail completely all such necessities; to record and then satisfy every one of these needs. And Thoth has laid bare these mysteries and made known all cries.

Serpents, guardians, ba-souls. The deities themselves have known every expression of every wish by which safe passage is ensured; and known, too, the reason why the hours have progressed, gates been opened and fiends kept at bay. This then, the encompassing knowledge; all to respond, all to know the wisdom of the god.

In this way, these passages and the gentle separation of Seker and the lord Re. The saving of the bright illumination, the preservation for the coming bright day.

Three doors in the entranceway in the rock face: Slitter-of-the-burial, Slitter-of-the-new-arm and Slitter-of-eternity and with the wisdom of Thoth, the right choice will be made. With wisdom, each correct description to be announced to the guardians, fiends, the ba-souls themselves. The recollections recorded in stone: the named ones, still ones, those that feed upon their own cries; feed upon fire itself. These summaries, these recollections will make any door open wide, make the need inevitable and the outcome too. All to be the subject of rejoicing so that the sun-god proceeds - and in the darkness, the hope of the multitudes, the warmth of the coming day.

The remnants of Amemet's hunger crumble in the first passageway - are sheltered from the fire issuing from the mouth of The Devourer. Burnt and dry husks - these consumed ones have about them the twisted gestures of those who have realized their own guilt at last - and fearfully so too.

The hall behind the entranceway shows charred figures lying piled on top of each other - broken and torn. Into the distance - piled with ashes till the far figures are indistinct in the haze - these figures are leant in mounds against the walls, they are piled to the ceiling. They are still, silent. Only occasionally a broken limb or the charred remains of a bone will topple and fall. The silence then will return.

Amemet, Devourer of souls in the Hall of the Double Maat; Amemet of Osiris' terrible judgement of the dead; of the forty-two assessor gods; Amemet of the scales of Thoth. And great god, Re, avert your gaze, leave behind corruption, the smallest trace of imperfection; all remnants of despair! Re, lord of the sun to rise in the morning above the land of Egypt; you sail in the solar barque in the clear air above!

Two doors remain. From where the wind issues, disturbing the sand, trickles of sound emerge. The second passageway is dark, but from within there are whispers, sounds of slithering on dry rock, on sand - and the air itself is heated and dried.

The frequent passage of air parches all moisture from damp surfaces, all tissues shrivel in this draught. Flames fanned by the air from the entranceway burn brighter - and there can be no moisture on the lips, no tears, no recollection of seas lapping on muddy coastlines. Here the frequent currents of air burn, burn.

No Nile flood. The drying desert; sand for ten thousand years, land of no life growing; and the desert of the heated air swirls in dry storms.

Down this channel are the currents of drying air to wither every drop, cause the river of the Underworld to shrivel and body tissue to die on the spot.

The wings. The beat of serpent wings and the wind echoes from the depths. It is Seker of death, the cry of the lord; Seker-who-is-on-his-sand and the wings move over his land, dry and shrivel all that might live, and the dead air then twists in the tunnels, echoes in the passageway. Flee, before the sound of the god's cry!

One respite remains. Here, there can be refuge from the darkest night, from the dark night fears. The sun-god is now to enter the third gate alone, and the ba-souls that would attend him and The Steersman and the maiden of this hour; all then depart. The solar lord will proceed down corridors alone. The light from this lord will parch and scar the surfaces of rocks and the journey is to approach the still turning point of the night; the silent centre in the land of Seker.

Invisible. In darkness; in channels in the rocks, in corridors - passageways where the spirits gesture in the night, unseen even by the lord of the sun. What image is this? What then from behind pillars, in silence, shadow, in concealment? And the journey to safety, to the beginning of things; the day to commence, and the transformations to begin.

In this way, in the depths of the night, the living god of the sun is to meet the sisters to the lord of the Duat, the Judge of the Dead.

And the birth of the day will commence.

Chapter Seventeen

THE GODDESS OF THE MOUNT

The serpent-boat is pulled up the mound, Khepri
envelops the goddess, origin of the dawn.

The fifth hour: The kingdom of Seker. Re enters the rock-cut channel: the passage is close to Seker - winding, rising and falling; and the inhabitants are seen only darkly in the shadows. This channel is separated from that through which the roar of Amemet might be heard. Though these passages weave among each other - a web within a web - they are unknown to each other and unknown to that channel of dry air through which the lord's cry might be heard. In the rock then these faint reverberations and the figures in the dark at the edge of vision, the *Baiu-amu-Duat;* these figures tremble. The path of Re then is never to meet the Lord-who-is-on-his-sand. Re passing through the dark reaches on a land boat formed from a serpent body itself is to see by the flames from its opened mouth. This serpent-boat then is pulled by the gods of the days of the month and by the sovereign chiefs: The-master-of-protection, The-bringer-of-pieces, Way-of-the-double-ruler and White-of-staff.

Heave, heave! Upward and upon each slope of sand. In the darkness: the mound, an unseen mountain; no wind or rain at all but the dry air instead of the unchanged Duat.

The sand mountain in the Underworld. Darkness. By these gods' great efforts the boat will reach to the still summit. In the shadows there the indistinct form penetrating from the very peak: the eyes, dressed hair, the torque about the neck; pale skin, the breathing head where no limbs or figure are to be seen. The eyes to see the approach of the god on the serpent boat and to stare into the darkness, the shape itself one vast promontory on the mount of the sands.

The mount of the Underworld reaches to the very cavern roof where rock processes form fingers pointing downwards; the form of the head buried nearly completely - for sand trickles down the slope whenever a breath is taken or the head turns to see - to see the face of the approaching lord.

Between the rock-fingers hanging above, shadows move and the longest projections pass from side to side. Others grow in length. The sounds of the approaching lord cause the form of a descending black and waxen head to appear. The reflections of certain small shining parts; the forelimbs, moving mouth-parts; the giant head of the scarab; scarab of dawn, the rise of the god, birth of the god. The sunrise in the dark. The descending scarab reaching down, larger now than the prisoner of the sand; in beauty, the face of the goddess. The greatest forelimbs now touching her hair; the legs soon to surround the head and the eyes: now to reflect back the light from the god of the sun, the sun from the two lands above.

Khepri, the dawn. Incomplete. The image in the Duat of the hope to come and the serpent-boat of Re moves

150

nearer and nearer the unknown head, goddess, unnamed lady of the kingdom of Seker. The scarab beetle above now envelops eyes, cheeks, lips and mouth; the forelimbs flick over the nose, onto the tongue. Hair is obscured: nothing then is to remain. Invisible this silent form: the goddess trapped, unspeaking - the acceptance of the advance of dawn.

And the advance of the Flesh-of-Re. The form of silence, the union of structures beyond imagining, forms of the god. The gentle gesture of the burning divine life - and the changing harbinger of light, union of the manifestations of light. The great god and the caress, the union of all three. Trinity on the sand of He-who-is-upon-his-sand. Under the earth, the first growth and an origin of the day itself. In the depths of this night, in the darkest moments, darkest realm, in the land of he who is the god's despair; in the sand made fertile in the darkness, in acceptance and in the union with the dead light; in this - beauty - the origin of the dawn.

The lord of the bright sun of the day, the dead lord, Flesh-of-Re, approaching the summit will burn, look into the rise of the sun. In darkness this beginning and Khepri will join Flesh-of-Re, indistinguishable - and there will be the first stirrings. The germ, ovum of life, seed of the day and in union the gods will bring hope for pulsing, turning, sheltering forms. The procession begins and the lady of the Duat - of women - beholds the origin, the infinitesimal spot, bright light in remote darkness.

There! There to persist in the night, and the changes to be welcomed. The circulations, breathing movements; flexures of muscles. All will develop and the processes begun in dark entrails of the night will never stop. Such processes will continue in the Duat, with the Flesh-of-Re, who will pass through caverns. Nothing now is to remain completely unchanged: the invisible, still dark day is within. A spark, at the summit at last.

The Flesh-of-Re in the serpent boat is pulled downwards on the slope of sand of He-who-is-upon-his-sand and moves towards the opening gates of the realm of Osiris, lord.

Chapter Eighteen

THE CRY OF OSIRIS

*Osiris revives, the god's murder recalled, the cry
forms Seker-on-his-sand.*

Osiris, the greater lord. Osiris betrayed and Osiris preserved. Osiris rising above the despair, above Seker-on-his-sand; what greater life, greater force than this? Can this lord ever be permanently broken, will not the life arise, the vigour become connected; will not aspiration, indignation emerge through veins and the connecting viscera: the flickering eyelids, the flickering awareness; the growth of muscle within muscle - the fractured bones to join, the sounds and sights to be observed in living eyes; the growth and flexure of longer muscles in back and leg; movements, at last, of eyelids and of the mouth? The evil to be perceived, and the breath to enter the body?

Rising; the arm, leg, phallus; the breath echoing in cavities within the chest and the arousal of hunger, growth, need; the recollection of whispers. The god will cause all resurrection in the Nile, the flooding and new vegetable growth - green.

Green, the colour of the forest before the deserts, a recollection of the life before death and of the face of

Osiris, the lord of vegetation, of growth - and of his rebirth itself.

The god Osiris, aroused from death. What strength is this? Can any force supersede? Would not such an essence rise from the dead sand in the heat of the day, rise from sulphur lakes, rise from fire, from the lion's mouth?

The mind glimmers: the sounds and searing heat, burning flesh. The cool water flowing over each limb, the smallest vibration through the ground, the sound of hard breathing and the knowledge then of the depths of evil, of the darkest act; the effort to extinguish the delicate vision; light in Egypt, the direction in the future of men, of rebirth and of the rise of new life - and of hope. Hope in the sun, hope in the growth from small seeds and eggs in the warmed waters, the swirling eddies which trap the essences, give rise to the growth of the new; to flowers.

To this death and the trickle of dried sand no wind at all: the dry husk of treachery; the burning air drawn suddenly inwards, the hiss of disturbed desires; the rattle of disjointed gestures, of the inescapable loss, the absence of one wish and then another; the steady accumulation of the lusts, loves, hates and needs. And the greatest moments become suffused in red blood, in bile, in *excreta.* Every foetid moment and the swirling heat prickles: no comfort; over dynasties no repose; the twisting, turning - and Seth's anger is to move rocks and open caves, to break open seals, to cause strange reflections in the surfaces of polished rocks.

The lord of the southern kingdom is able to burn the barks of palms and leaves of trees by his look: vegetable growth consumed in haste by his glance. The rivers dry: red, the sand flows and the rocks melt to glasses - these then form the cavities where new minerals vaporize in the heat. Seth of lust; lustful warrior of envy, of anger, of hatred, of the seventy-two conspirators. The feast for brother Osiris is laid and the trap is set. And the wagers and the wine; the food and the dear brother Osiris, home:

Brother Osiris, for the wager, enter this casket! See! It will fit, fit perfectly . . . !

The lid closed, the seals made fast - and the god inside is betrayed.

Osiris screams and the echoes then penetrate the earth, they are driven into passages and channels. The sound reverberates in the caverns and hours of the Duat; the god's scream forever.

The cry echoes as the god dies, echoes as the casket is thrown by Seth into the Nile. The closed channels of the Duat are to preserve the sound for the hours, days and years - echoing still, undiminished, and the casket floats through the delta to the sea, to Gubla.

What remains are the echoes - and the reverberation disturbs the centuries' dust in the channels of dust. Of sand - sand of ages moved and disturbed: fearful shapes formed and the echoes mount. The shapes stir, the sand *becomes* these processes; is sculpted by the sound and it becomes the *moving* forms - flowing as the scorpion of sand moves - as the seventeen-headed Menmenu of sand roams in the channels. These tread the dark kingdom and live by the dying gasps of souls who might venture there.

But the figure sculpted most fearsomely by the disturbing influence of eternal echoes; the form built through ages into first a slight protuberance and then a contour, was constructed into a moving figure - as the echoes made their circling dance through the channels of the Duat. This frame reflected the despairing cycle: onwards ever onwards, with serpent wings below catching the subtle flow of air currents; these then moving and deflecting air - air and the despairing cry itself. The figure indeed was formed *by the god's cry*: the man-figure, the serpent and the wings moving in darkness – never formed in the sun, unknown to all daytime moments, given only to the variety of night-time fears, to the darkness, to despair.

The cry: Seker himself. Seker of sand: Seker-upon-his-sand!

Chapter Nineteen

THE HALL OF THE DOUBLE MAAT

*Osiris becomes Judge of the Dead, the goddess Maat,
the ba of Hor enters the hall.*

Seth, in this way, consigned his brother Osiris to the deep: darkness, the despair, echoes and the night.

But the love of the truest sister was to revive the life of Osiris, to create Horus - the principle of kingship - Horus, pharaoh of pharaohs in the day and the light. Isis, sister and wife, was able to follow the casket over the sea.

And the union then of the noble lord, Osiris, with the tree of Gubla: Osiris to become the king of the Underworld, the Judge of the Dead. Osiris! Osiris of the night.

———

The sixth hour - of the lord of the dead in the hall of the double Maat - Hor in the company of the assessor gods, in the shadow of the scales of Thoth.

Maat: ordered, the sweetness of all harmonies. The direction of the will and the desires of all men.

The desires accumulate and the hopes increase: the protection of soldiers, the ordering of the motions of the stars and the moon. Rightness and justice are in the glance of the Horus-god on earth. The pharaoh's will has made the land prosper - and the grain is then stored high in jars.

Pharaoh among the gods and the order of the land is governed by the rise of the Nile itself, the growth of Hapi: the order of rains in highlands. The sun will turn - and from the four corners: Hapy, Imsety, Duamutef, Qebehsenuef winds will raise the sand and the sun will dry the corn. There will be storms of the invisible one on the sands, Min erect in the desert; there will be the guardianship of Seth and the beauty of loyal sisters: Isis, Nephthys. The gods themselves in their order: beauty and rightness. There will be wonder and balancing desires.

This vision of Maat: correctness, harmony itself - the vision glimpsed only now and then. Maat, Maat, Maat herself. Serene goddess: of the plume; of the outstretched arms. Maat: order, beauty, shining light. Guide of the ways: the truth of the journey, truth of the path.

Daughter Maat! Father Re approaches this path and the stars turn and the light slips through the heavens. The moon and the planets pass precisely and are recorded forever, are known to Thoth. The gentle passage is then to be plotted, each meeting recorded and the fates of all to be imagined: to turn towards Maat, to hear Thoth, to be guided by truth and knowledge and the recording of words.

Thoth and Maat will guide the god and judge mankind. Maat in the temple of Montu, present then at Waset; and the lightness of the plume is to be the touch of truth recorded by Thoth. Truth of mind, knowledge, enquiry and the record. Thoth: guide, in the hall of judgement at last!

And in the hall the balance is about to be prepared. Down echoing passages the sound of approaching forms. They are the ba-souls from the setting of the sun, they have journeyed - a fluttering crowd about the form of Re - from the mountain at Manu. Bodies mouth-opened, ba-souls prepared for the journey - and with each proper word to be spoken, each guardian's name known - they have entered each gate and every hour of the Duat. They have passed with safety to this hall; and the serpents' fiery breath and the jaws of Apopis and the lake of fire have not consumed them. And they have passed through this territory of the dead; and Seker, the cry of Osiris, has not stopped their hearts with the lord's torment.

We have suffered. In the kingdom of the two lands we have died amid lamentations, died alone, died with screams of pain and with the gasps of every exhausted moment to echo about mud-brick rooms and about palaces.

Lives in contemplation, in praising your name. Brave lives and attacks upon the most fearful foes. Lives spent and each observance completed, each votive offering made: we are of loyal service to the pharaoh; have struggled for the pharaoh's repose, struggled on journeys for the rarest oils, we have died in our efforts - in foreign lands, on the journey to Punt, returning from Punt.

And Hor among us has completed every task. Hor, priest of Montu, gatherer of oils, opener of the gates at Waset, son of Ankhori and son of Karem; Hor at one with Horus and Thoth, enshrined with Atum and carried to the cemetery with the Apis bull, Hor dead, oh Hor dead. Hor, drowned in the river.

The last breath. Breath of the dry wind of the desert, the wind over the fields and from among dwellings and temples, from the dust of roads; this air from home, this air from the birth chamber, nursery and the scribes' rooms, the temple precinct - hot sun in the inner courtyard - and the air blows through reeds by the river. And birds fly, soar in the desert air. Sweet air.

Recorded by Thoth are the exhortations, divine rites, memories of holy offices and the obeisances to the lord, the lord!

The spasm which will fail, the eyes which will turn upward: the last motion of arm and shoulder. Hor, dead, dead - drowned in Hapi, drowned in the Nile.

The ba of Hor floats nearer still. Down passages the essential light flies and fears are screamed out.

The judgement scene from the sixth hour of the sun-god's journey through the Underworld. It shows Anubis weighing the heart against the feather of truth (Maat). Thoth records the outcome and the whole is presided over by Osiris (seated) with Isis and Nephthys standing behind.

The image on the front cover is from the Book of the Dead and shows a detail from this scene. Here the four sons of Horus appear in front of Osiris above a lotus bloom.

Chapter Twenty

THE JUDGEMENT OF HOR

Hor professes his innocence, the scales weigh his heart against the feather of Maat, the Assessor Gods give their verdict.

In the dim light in the cavern the outline of the scales is visible only in the brightness from the doorway to the god's chamber.

The ba equipped with each chosen word: the properly prepared one. Hor with the name of each guardian of every cavern, of the terrors in each region of the Duat; the ba prepared, passing in clouds of luminescence, absorbing the heat, reflecting the light. And the multitude of ba-souls dead on that day have come with Re from Manu and the sunset itself. These companions, these attenders, these supplicants, these figures in torment, these terrified remnants: cries in the night, fears in the night; these essences wait in the corridors silently, wait with Hor, wait for the Judgement of the Double Maat.

The death after death and the roars of Amemet are heard all the while. Devourer, not yet visible, the roars echo and the ba-souls tremble: for each spirit of mobility the demonstration of *innocence* itself. And the forty-two assessor gods seated above must grant their acquiescence: to each a denial - or the soul's blood will be drunk.

That nothing might exist! Vacuity, the absence; no blame, no lust, no greed, no defilement, no theft, no sacrilege; no burdens carried unknown throughout the night. In sleep no terrors, no moments and hours in anguish. Can such as these be sustained? Can the torments be denied, will no reckoning occur?

The persistence of evil. Evil in the iridescence of insects' wings. In carapaces. In the gels, oozes, slimes of decay; in the flesh: the destruction of all body functions and the slow descent. Disorder.

Oh Maat, Maat! Save and succour!

The planets move correctly. Your order and the Nile is fertile, the winds blow freely, justly in the heat of the desert day: the winds over the sands, the paths over the earth.

Govern this excess. To the Terrible-of-faces, to The Flame, to the Crusher-of-bones; to Him-with-his-face-behind-him.

I tremble, Maat, before the assessor gods:

Oh Far-strider, who came forth from Iunu, I have done no falsehood.
Oh Fire-embracer, who came forth from the Kherga, I have done no robbery.

Oh Swallower-of-shades who came forth from the cavern, I have not stolen.

Oh Dangerous-one, who came forth from Rosetjau, I have not killed men.

Oh Double-lion who came forth from the sky, I have not destroyed food supplies.

Oh Eyes-of-fire who came forth from Khem, I have done no crookedness.

Oh Flame-which-comes-forth-backwards, I have not stolen the god's offerings.

Oh Bone-breaker who came forth from Henensu, I have not told lies.

Oh Green-of-flame who came forth from Memphis, I have not taken food.

Oh Eater-of-entrails who came forth from the House of Thoty, I have not committed perjury.

Oh Lord-of-truth, who came forth from Maat, I have not stolen bread.

Oh Wanderer who came forth from Bubastis, I have not eavesdropped.

Oh Wementi-snake who came forth from the place of execution, I have committed no homosexuality.

Oh Disturber who came forth from Weryt, I have not been easily angered.

Oh Youth who came forth from the Yunu Nome, I have not been deaf to the truth.

Oh You-whose-face-is-behind-you, who came forth from the cavern of Wrong, I have not misconducted myself nor copulated with a boy.

Oh Hot-foot who came forth from the darkness, I have not been quarrelsome.

Oh Owner-of-faces who came forth from Nedjefet, I have not been impatient.

Oh Accuser, who came forth from Wetjenet, I have not transgressed my nature, I have not washed at the picture of a god.

Oh Owner-of-horns, who came forth from Asyat, I have not been voluble in speech.

Oh Nefertum, who came forth from Memphis, I have seen no evil.

Oh Temsep, who came forth from Busiris, I have not made conjuration against the pharaoh.

Oh You-who-acted-according-to-your-will, who came forth from Tjebu, I have not waded in water.

Oh Commander-of-mankind, who came forth from your house, I have not reviled God.

Oh Bestower-of-powers, who came forth from the city, I have not made distinctions for myself.

Oh Serpent-with-raised-head, who came forth from the cavern, I am not wealthy except with my own property.

Oh Serpent-who-brings-and-gives, who came forth from the Silent Land, I have not blasphemed God in my city.

The light shone on the forty-two shrines, on the seated forms, animal forms, the rigid, mummiform essences: they are hawk-headed, they are of the ram, the jackal, ibis, cow, lion, frog; they are man-headed. The deities who listen; the silent figures, judges, the assessors are moved to pronounce: pronounce knowledge of all losses, deceptions, the breaking of promises and the fear, fear of the darkness in defeated eyes, the fragrances of deceit. In the dark, false promises and in the dust and still air, a resolve. Hor in the Underworld to live; Hor to die. The *second death* to confront the soul; limbs to be torn apart. Amemet crushing, devouring, and this darkness now forever.

Dust, for the thousand-times truthful: settling throughout centuries. The cascades of dust with the inclination of each head, the slightest movement of head and shoulders. Anger, anger of the gods.

Hor will tremble. The moments of a life spent piously and in discord now appear broken into crystal: each glinting surface brings light of a different colour, blending and merging. An essence that turns joy into disturbance, the beating of the heart into tremors and tears.

And the bald statement of innocence dazzles the watchers; brings about, by brilliance alone, by their own reflections and remnant images: an outcome. Will the heart be wanting, weighed down at all; weighed down with the mortal, the venial, the too terrible to behold?

The heart in the balance. Hor's heart against the feather of Maat. Anubis reaches upward to each scale-pan in the dim light. The heart will be weighed against truth itself. The heart at each dawn; for every summer of his life; the heart as companion to each day, to the rivalries of night, the blackness of each fear.

The scale settles. In the distance now, The Devourer, Amemet. The beast hungers and roars.

Moments of sanctity, moments of piety. The heart overfilling and the trembling feather of Maat descending; rising. The waves on the sea, the flicker of eyes in bright

166

sunlight, the moments summed - of birth and conflict, of the love of rare and beautiful things.

The desert, men's avarice and the small perversions of beauty and innocence. Will every moment so add and none subtract? The feather rises and Amamet breathes faster, shakes the many parts - hippopotamus, crocodile, lion - of which the Devourer is made; breathes again, lunges forward for the hand, leg, the head of Hor.

Blood, blood to flow and the soul to be devoured - the second death. But the assessor gods each move imperceptibly and the figure of Thoth, close to the scales, moves too, and the first air movements in so many years twist into eddies. The dust of the ages turns upward in air, exposing amulets and scarabs, the bright forms of the deities themselves. The air swirls, the feather flutters, the scale pans settle.

No movement, no final movement at all. To the gods their judgement: the priest of Montu, the opener of the gates of heaven at Waset, son of Ankhori and son of Karem remains to breathe the dust-filled air in the dark cavern. *Hor remains to journey inwards in these realms of origins and of endings.*

And now the moment will come when face to face with the mightiest of lords, lord of the night-time kingdom; the suffering lord of dismemberment; lord of the tree at Gubla, the screaming lord - in death the lord, the father. (And the fleeting form of Horus rises overhead to settle behind the pharaoh, to protect the king. The lord of darkness cries out and the echo moves amid the silences of the Duat. The echo then shapes and forms Seker-on-his-sand and Osiris rules, rules in the night-time kingdom.)

Despair is thus banished, the lord of this darkness is to be approached at last.

Hor speaks:

Oh you who are uplifted on your standard, lord of the Atef crown, who made your name as lord of the wind, save me from your messengers.

I have seen the rejoicings in the land of the Fenkhu.

What did they give you?

A fire brand and a pillar of faience. I buried them on the river bank of Maat.

Come and enter by this door of the Hall of Justice - for you know us.

But the door remains barred and words from the doorway itself drift upwards towards Hor - only barely able to be heard.

Whispers:

We will not let you enter unless you tell our name.

Fall-of-truth, is your name.

From the floor itself these words can now be heard:

I will not let you pass by me, unless you tell my name.

Ox-of-Geb is your name.

I will not let you enter by me! Whispers come from the hasp of the door.

Living-Eye-of-Sobek, Lord-of-Bakhu, is your name.

From the door itself:

I will not open to you unless you tell my name.

Breast-of-Shu which is placed as a protection for Osiris, is your name.

From the cross-timbers:

We will not let you enter unless you tell our names.

Children-of-uraei, are your names.

I will not let you enter by me, says the door-keeper of the Hall of Justice, *unless you tell my name.*

Knower-of-hearts, searcher-out-of-bodies, is your name.

To which God shall I announce you?

To him who is now present, tell it to the interpreter of the two lands.

Come! Says Thoth. *What is your condition?*

I am pure from evil.

To whom shall I announce you?

Announce me to Him whose roof is of fire, whose walls are of living serpents and the floors of whose house are the waters - to Osiris, lord.

Proceed: what goes forth at the voice for you upon earth is the Sacred Eye.

Chapter Twenty-one

THE FIELD OF REEDS

Osiris and the Sons of Horus, Hor meets the Bennu bird in the Field of Reeds.

The door opens, the light streams outward. In the light beneath the earth four figures are to be seen, lotus-borne, blossoming, they are the pillars of the sky; the cardinal directions from which winds may come; they are sons of Horus; guardians of the viscera: of the lungs, liver, stomach; the entrails. The figures move - shadows in the bright light - Hapy, Imsety, Duamutef, Qebehsenuef. Light streams from the throne of the lord of the Duat, lord of the Atef crown, with crook and flail; of growth and rebirth. Osiris in green; Osiris, progenitor of Horus - of Isis, husband and brother; of Nephthys, brother and love.

The one broken lord, pharaoh. Lord: the two lands rejoice!

And paradise now - with Osiris in the Field of Reeds. What world of bright imaginings awaits? What lakes and waterways sparkle in the eternal light? The end of all suffering. For Hor, no fear then of the dark night in waiting, of the sun setting and the journey on the Barque of Re.

In your barge, Hor, visit the smaller, brightly-lit waterways; and the cry of the marsh birds and the sound of the insects will accompany you, for all hope is now present. Hope: the vision reflected in droplets on all leaves, on rushes. Images which beckon inwards. Each vision to be perceived in delight - on every surface, in specular highlights, in points of light. Images of every memory, every moment in the life spent and in the lives of others. In droplets by the banks; in the mists of morning; among the palms. In each instant - in the Field of Reeds, all other times. This paradise, this wonder, this confluence of beauty. And at every following moment, the future is of hope rewarded, assurances of the infinite reflections, reflected lives; instants and ages perceived in sparkling droplets; in iridescence; in the light on insects' wings.

There is hope of lives merging, each to be renewed by others yet more hope-filled. Within such lives more is reflected. They spin onwards. In every direction joy itself will increase unendingly.

Each fond imagining of the tillers of the fields; of the soldier in the heat - burning while death awaits - of the days and months of the sailor's thirst, of the danger of his abandonment; of the cries of the sea birds and salt air massing in storms away from land.

Oh the wonder of these sparkling points. On burnished bronze, on the white caps of waves at sea. In the birth-chamber, on jars, in oil-filled vessels - the light bright in points within. In the extremity: crying for the birth, screaming for light, air; for darkness to be taken away. On all such occasions these images within brilliants give, when seen through half-closed lids, when light itself is

172

too much to bear, the hint of possibilities within paradise, in the Field of Reeds - passions and joys fulfilled in the light.

But the pharaoh in the kingdom of the two lands once saw motion of a dark and disturbed form: the small crawling creatures repelled by paradise shifted and took up new positions whenever the eye was able to encounter them directly. In this way darkness was joined to the light.

And men could think, feel, dream, might bring forth sweetness and the death of each petal on the flowers of morning, flowers of evening; each bloom that might give fragrance to the night-time air. Each nature and simulacrum is thus represented and the pharaoh then would bring with him the darkness and the threat. In this way now, it is Hor who precedes him.

Hor in beauty. Hor in the repose of the Field of Reeds. Hor: the land of the dead lord and water passages - perpetual waters - that ripple and drift, which form wavelets and eddies. Upon these the sparkles of eternal sunlight so that in these brilliants the images of dreams and hopes are displayed and in the movement of the reeds in the bright sunlight the shifts of hope become displayed. Nothing, nothing, then of joy to be excluded - and one might then see the greatest paradise of all.

Hor in his barge amid the reeds will visit every part; pass over every island, travel down every waterway. And the barge of Hor glides over ripples which give rise to the ocean: warm waters and the heated passages through enclosed channels. And in the widest seas even cold currents move. There ocean beasts dwell. These beasts: no legs, no feet, their tails thrash in the foam and the sunlight. There are essences and recollections in every brilliant droplet: from the oar, from the low, flat barge, the reed-bed river mouth; and in the brightest part of the day.

In the barge in the Field of Reeds, Hor will visit the great company of the gods: journey to the temple of the Field of Reeds. Hor will store the tall emmer and Hor will attend the three lakes: Qetqet, The-two-great-gods and Offerings-of-peace, and the priest of Montu then will approach the Bennu bird. The fragrances of flowers will follow Hor and all good and pure things will follow too - in offerings - and the streams of the Field of Reeds are wide so that the distance between their banks can never be known. And in such streams no serpents, no pursuit at all.

And by the island which stretches the length of this heaven - the temple. The temple! Birthplace of the god.

On the island of the great company of the gods, an ascent and in the boat, Tcheterfet, too, stairs rise, lead upwards from the domain of Neith. In this Field of Reeds, is found unknown beauty of dreams in every mote in the air.

Hor approaches the Bennu bird. Bright rays rising: the bird beyond the eastern horizon. The wings now outstretched as the sun's fingers reach out: the morning light, a remembrance of the red sky above the wide sea. This creature of the dark sea beneath is to rise like the sun in rays stabbing outwards: red, which will touch the tops of the mountains at dawn. The wonder, the bird in the Field of Reeds, and Hor's hand reaches out to touch:

I have soared; I have become Khepri. I have grown as plants grow. I am the fruit of every god. I am the seventh of the seven cobras who come into being in the west. I have come by day, dawning in the footsteps of the gods. I am Khonsu who cuts the throats of the lords.

Khonsu and the red blood of morning flows. The Bennu bird rises above the water. Beyond the eastern horizon: too early, it is day. Red light touches the mountain tops in the sky.

Fly, make the sky your repose. Above the horizon your flight from the east, your life eternal: in the air, the movement of every wingstroke; the reflection then of the hope in the Field of Reeds.

Chapter Twenty-two

FLESH-OF-OSIRIS

Apopis attacked by the scorpion goddess, Flesh-of-Re approaches the four spirit-forms of Osiris.

The great god Flesh-of-Re enters Osiris' hidden abode: the seventh hour of the Duat.

The Barque of Re aground, and the trickle of marshy water swirls beneath the keel - what now to help in the progress of the god?

Ahead, the writhing neck and head of the serpent Neha-hra, like Apopis, it will block the way, threaten the wonder of Re. And Apopis is the darkness which surrounded the Nun before creation began. Apopis: enemy of the light, encircler of the Nun and of the god of light within.

In the shallow water the serpent undulates. Oh Serquet, scorpion goddess and divine one, Master-of-his-knives, seize the serpent! Transfix these coils to the river-bed with your knives. Save, save the passage of the lord!

Goddesses: Uniter, Offerer, Copulator and Destroyer - with your knives, hack Apopis. Cut, slice and kill the serpent and protect, oh, save the spirit-forms of the lord! Osiris of four forms, Osiris in the hidden abode.

But Isis, Great-of-magic, now enters the Barque of Re. Isis was able to revive even the broken lord, to flutter bird wings above the corpse and raise in this way desire - desire from the dead. Thus was Horus engendered in the union of the living and the dead. Isis now in the prow commands the barque with no water beneath. Isis commands the barque itself:

Proceed towards Osiris of these spirit-forms.

The dead form of Osiris, Flesh-of-Osiris, seated, wears the sky-god crown and is protected by the serpent, Life-of-maker-of-offerings. The evil done by men is now to be destroyed before his eyes.

Silence, silence in the secret abode, for the goddesses protect what the gentle, dead eyes regard: lovingly, longingly the god's flesh and the god's forms. Four temples of Osiris recumbent, and Flesh-of-Osiris sees the desire of Isis for the corpse - and thus four temples to the forms of the god are to be illuminated by Re.

Re passes. The Barque of Re, now floating above dry sand, shines with the brilliance of the sun-god. Dry heat and the passage of Re: the searing light - and at each cornice of the temple roofs, the movement of dark and indistinct shapes. The first appearance then of eyes, mouths - and of inclined heads. Each then turning to face the unaccustomed sun. From fissures in the walls and roofs, from between pillars and underneath eaves, the heads and faces appear. Each turns towards the sound of Re's voice as he addresses the guardians of each of the forms of the lord Osiris.

The heads projecting from the corners and interstices make expressions of agreement, they show concern for the safety of their charges - and each then slowly gives his assent.

The Barque of Re glides on as shadows lengthen over the four temples of Osiris. As the dark begins to return, the heads move to face each other and silently, bloodily they begin to eat their own forms.

In this hidden abode, Osiris' pleasure is to have union with his spirit-forms: such silent joy while the ba of Hor floats in the Field of Reeds.

More, before the united Osiris, in the eyes of Re too there is the elevation of the just. The great currents of these spirits, their flights of hope. The space becomes filled and the light of Re moves on - moves to the company of gods, moves higher still, moves towards the stars: harbingers, bringers of an end to things. Light after the dawn.

The Maidens of the Hours cry out. The crocodile beast: Osiris-The-Eye-Of-Re, protector of the tomb of Osiris, is to become enchanted by the words of Re. The dead form of Osiris rises. Dead god, Osiris lord, lord of the Atef crown.

The figure of Hor moves in a low, flat boat in the waters of paradise while the Barque of Re leaves the regions of Osiris' cry, of Osiris' Judgement, of the hidden abode of Osiris, lord. Re, in the eighth hour of his journey in the Duat moves to meet Ptah-Tatenen and the gods who are held within the ten balconies of the Duat.

Chapter Twenty-three

THE GODS IN THE BALCONIES

The partially dead, Flesh-of-Re visits the balconies of the Duat.

Over the naos-canopy on the Barque of Re the snake, Mehen, shields Flesh-of-Re, coils above Flesh-of-Re. Mehen commands and the gods obey, they tow the barque into the eighth hour of the journey through the Duat.

Avengers of the god Re; followers of Osiris line the cavern walls. Their cries are of the eternally imprisoned, for their preserved forms have stood silently in rows - they live, but they live only in their heads. Death has come partially to these followers of the gods, they cry out: living heads upon dead and mummified bodies. Prisoners of their bodily desiccation. These unbandaged heads free from natron move as their eyes follow the passage of the god. Their bodies remain stiff, dead, decaying slowly over the ages: they cry out in rejoicing at the passage of their lord. Their desperate cries may be heard in the kingdom of the two lands where they cause all enemies of Re to be seized, and with knives burnished with the rays of this sun, they cause the heads of enemies in profane revolt to be severed from their bodies.

In love and loyalty to the sun-god himself, these followers of Osiris praise his name as the bright light falls upon them. As the Barque of Re departs, the living heads on the dead bodies cry out their despair after the departing lord. Their eyes are left staring out into the darkness that remains. Slowly then beneath their heads, their bodies desiccate in the dry air, crumble at the extremities, become eaten into by insects in each layer of their bandages, they fracture and then break apart with the ages.

By the sides of the river, amid dust and broken rock, standing out from rock faces and from inside cave entrances, under cliffs and cut from the rock surface itself, the forms of balconies are projecting. Their doors are sealed - no light, no sound; the silent movement of shards among cascades of rock fragments. Silence and the waves lap on the banks beneath.

The door to the first balcony opens it is named now as Slitter-lord. The light from the Barque of Re, from the Flesh-of-Re himself penetrates to the back and burns into the rock. What little moisture remaining there in woodwork, in the dry offerings on low tables, in incense, in the dried-out vessels, rises indistinctly as vapour.

From the balcony a low whirring begins. From one end of the alcove to the centre; then from the centre to the side, the slight noise travels in and out of shadow. At first it is blocked off by the image at the centre - the image of Atum of the descending sun.

There is, too, the image of the god of the light, Shu. Shu of the air; Shu, of the single soul with Tefnut, Shu who dispersed the darkness at the time of chaos; Shu, feather-light; Shu, of the wind.

And at the end of the balcony: the giant scarab worked in stone. Khepri, image of the dawn, recollection of the land of Seker; and from these three images themselves, a cry towards Re.

The sound from the balcony is of the beating of insects' wings, the hum of bees: the cry, unvoiced, of a million invisible flying forms. From still mouths, with no breath, the images of the three gods call out to Re, praise the sun-god, Re - and with that, their door closes peremptorily to conceal these forms.

Slitter-raised-by-Ptah-Tatenen, the door of the second balcony opens: within there is the sound of weeping, weeping.

Women in despair, women in pain and the light from the Barque of Re picks out effigies in stone: of Tefnut, Geb and of Nut.

Tefnut of the mists with Geb, her son of the earth. And always there has been love, love to grow! For the earth will be moved, the rich soil of Egypt will meet the sky. Nut, beautiful maiden of the sky, Nut: body in starlight. Nut will arch over the earth: no space at all but instead the beauty of love with Geb amid the stars. Nut, transfixed in joy. Stars and the passage of the sun itself from birth to its decline. The divine form.

Sorrow for Tefnut and jealousy for the divine form. For Shu loved Tefnut and daughter Nut as well. In anger was Shu to place the greatest space between the lovers: the earth reclining and the sky so arched. Winds, the air, space itself, to come between.

Tefnut of sorrows! Women! Women, then weep!

Women, weep!

181

The third door, Slitter-unknown-to-souls, opens with the moaning of great men. The deeply indrawn breath of nights of splendour spent in torment. The pharaoh's cries in the heat of the night. And within the shade, taller than any man, higher than the walls of monuments to dead kings; capable of blocking out all else from the sun, moon, the stars stand the figures in stone - of Osiris lord, of Isis, and of the son, Horus. Horus, lord of the two lands and the one true issue of both the living and the dead. Isis, the mother - and the great love has passed from death to the living.

The fourth door opens in a darker part of the cavern, the river now flows stronger, and the sounds from those images within are more distant still. So little is seen in the shadowed recesses that the names of these gods - names set in hieroglyphs, surrounded by cartouches - are all that might distinguish the dimly-lit forms within: Bull-of-the west, Soul-of-the-gods and Tears-of-the-gods reply to Re and the sound is of men lamenting and of the bellows of a bull.

The fifth door, Slitter-and-uniter-of-darkness, preserves within more forms. They are the images of Khetery, Ifefy and Iranbefy but here the darkness is so deep the doors themselves cannot be seen when they open and within, the cries of the gods are of pleading - pleading made in terror.

Behind a pillar, so large it obscures a side-channel to the cavern, the shadows stretch out into endless space. Nothing, nothing can be seen in the shadow but from there the sound of water can be heard tumbling in cascades down a rock face unseen.

Cries from other balconies on the walls out of sight can be heard. Behind the door, Slitter-of-the-shoulder-of-the-earth, the unknown gods cry out with the sounds of a host of cats while behind Slitter-of-the-enemies-of-Re, the seventh door, the sounds are of men living happily by the Nile.

Slitter-powerful-of-form, the eighth door holds the muffled cries of men in battle: the clash of swords at the battle of Nu, these are the cries of men dying bloodily on the spot.

Behind Slitter-sharp-of-flame a host of the unknown cry out. Here is heard the hawk's call: Horus, the divine hawk, spirit at one with the pharaoh of the two lands.

The last balcony is just visible, though high up on the banks of the river's dark tributary. Within: the sound of the wings of waterfowl descending over a lake, or the sound - at a great distance - of the call of birds over a delta; the night-turning of fowl in flight; the moments in the dark when disturbances pass among birds preparing to leave at dawn. The door, Slitter-of-the-blessed-dead, partly visible, is open slightly and within can be seen the gods that create the sounds of the reed-bed delta in the dark:

Above the parapet, writhing and coiling cobra heads are raised, tongues flick forward, eyes stare. Behind, other uraei coil on linen nests far from sight:

Oh Re! You have visited your servants and believers, and silence, silence now overwhelms them! Your barque passes and with the fading of your light, the cries die away. The gods abandoned!

No sound, the silence of dust falling gently on all exposed surfaces:

Re passes the nine mummies, erect and guarding the corridor to the cavern of the ninth hour of the night.

Chapter Twenty-four

SHESSHES AND AAI

The goddesses who engender desire of Osiris for Isis, Shesshes and Aai grapple with Apopis who is harpooned.

The river is now deeper and the banks have no passageway at all, the Barque of Re must be rowed by Divine-of-the-gods, by Imperishable, Unwearying, Taster and the helpers who come with them. They raise their oars to pour water onto the parched figures in the dim light on either bank - in alcoves, on projecting rocks. Serpents coil, raise their heads and spit fire among themselves. The sulphurous fumes rise, the burning pools lie before the serpents and give rise to the small light in the ninth cavern, in the echoing space.

The serpents turn and coil among themselves; their breathing is like the rush of winds around swallow-holes, they illuminate only certain features: emblems, the glint of stones in collars and amulets. They pick out the features of only the nearest of the throng in the shadows. There are unseen figures pressing down to the banks of the river: the followers, the sufferers - the gods in the underworld; spirit-forms, those who wait in outer darkness to attend upon their lord.

Twelve female figures line the river - in shadow, they are barely to be seen. In the darkness, no breathing at all, but with the passage of the lord Re, the light falls upon each goddess in turn. The dust rises from shoulders, arms, breasts - and the first breath is taken. Shuddering, they chant in low unison.

The words echo round the cave and are able to make others incant. By their cries once, the desire of the dead god Osiris for Isis was revived as she fluttered above. By their cries also - the birth of Horus; by their cries, too, the lord Osiris rules:

In the darkness, raise the standard of the south; by the river of the Duat, raise the standard of the north.

The hawk-headed sphinx lies between gods of the two crowns, is surmounted by the twin-headed Horus-and-Seth, and The Opener walks with an eight-headed serpent. From the back of the serpent, Tepi, rise the heads of men - their arms raised in prayer.

On the far bank too, the creatures of the Duat attend their lord. The spirits of the Amentet walk behind, and there are followers, too, of Thoth, of Horus and Osiris - with heads of men, the heads of ibises, the heads of hawks, the heads of rams; each of whom pulls upon the rope which brings with it tangled and coiled serpents, crowned serpents - and serpents with legs writhing beneath their bodies too.

The Barque of Re steers between these river banks. Ahead, the water boils in disturbance as the snake-tailed crocodile, Shesshes, circles around Apopis; as the sound of water thrashing fills the cavern with fearsome echoes;

as the figures of men advance bearing grappling nets; as three harpoonists take aim, as the prostrate figure of Aai creeps forward towards the serpent of darkness; as Aai bears over his head the rope with which to grapple the enemy of Re; as all these figures attack the evil Apopis the Barque of Re glides safely and silently by - it glides past amid brilliants.

Apopis! The slaughtering places are against thee, and the ass-gods are against thee!

The figures with harpoons drive their weapons into Apopis and the Barque of Re is gone. Past the crocodile; past the loyal helpers with their nets; past the Maidens of the Hours; past Tepi; past Aai the glorious god Re moves silently on and passes then towards the gates of the tenth hour of the Duat.

Chapter Twenty-five

SETH

*The Hentiu slash Apopis, Geb and the Sons of Horus
hold him down, Seth assists Flesh-of-Re throughout
this hour, Mehen is carried away.*

Oh cavern of The-deep-well-of-the-river-banks! The
barque carries Re, the high god, into the dark centre and
Re is adored by sixteen serpents on the walls. Here, there
parade before the god the Hentiu with their knives and
ropes. At each step in their journey, their broad shoulders
shake and their feet resound. At their approach - each
with four heads, with the hissing, writhing, biting and
tearing heads of serpents - at their approach the red eyes
blaze, the tongues twist and the light of Re reflects upon
the serpent scales.

Here, the snake-headed men. Here the tangled
wriggling mass on the manly necks: here eyes dart in all
directions - to each sound the tongues flicker; they are
moving towards the greatest enemy of all. The blackness
surrounding the waters and the red of the blood from the
deepest wounds: in the water, throughout the caverns and
drifting with the flow of the river is the boiling blood of
the red-stained enemy himself. Evil triumphant, evil
brought low. Apopis, Apopis in chains! Apopis, serpent
in your agony now.

Turn, turn and your cry echoes beyond the cavern walls. Your cry flies before you!

At each turn of the huge body, each thrashing movement, the wounds and gashes to the body of the serpent expose the viscera inside. There are bloody new mouths opened and there are the white flashes of bone twisting inside flesh. Apopis still lives but in the gloom the sands shift suddenly:

A hand! A hand to hold down the chains to every coil of Apopis' body and the Hentiu move towards the captive itself.

The hand rising from the sand, bigger than the Sphinx at Giza, the hand to resemble the pyramids of well-remembered pharaohs. Rising from level ground it shakes free from the sand and grasps the chain about the body of Apopis; it wrestles, constrains - in this way it holds down evil for hearts to follow. Its shadow looms above the head of the serpent of the Duat and the face of the concealed body beneath remains forever hidden.

None but the gods may approach the raised head and gaping mouth: the breath and the cry of Apopis. And above the four gods: the Stefiu fight to hold down the chain along the length of the serpent's body, they fight and the scorpion goddess, Serquet, moves nearer and nearer the serpent's fangs. Geb, the earth, and the four pillars of the sky unite: they are Hapy, Imsety, Duamutef and Qebehsenuef. These figures spring from the chain which holds Apopis and thus the earth and the heavens join together in the depths, unite in the Duat:

All then, the heights and the earth beneath. Every vertical cliff; each pillar and temple wall; the cataract fall of water on the Nile; each cavern deep in the earth where the water will settle silently after ages - and shadows fall vertically at noon from travellers in the desert; from the sun amid storms in the desert, from the god of the storm, of rain descending. Potency, the power of night-time growth and Osiris causes the seed to germinate and the emmer to rise.

Iron, pillars of iron, the glint of metal rising upward. No limit to the columns in air. The sunlight too, in hope. Each gesture a movement to ascend, each moment an arching drift of winds.

Carried to the heavens: seeds, pollen, feathers and bright winged insects, the hawk ascending. With wings outstretched in the turning air, the hawk of the two lands rises above the death of the god.

Will the aerial path of the son of Osiris mark, pass unnoticed, or indicate the passage of water flowing to the sea, will it pass to the company of the living high god - burning - the presence, full light, bright light, bright sun of day?

Created, re-created, the light shines on high. The vertical path, the pillars: Hapy, Imsety, Duamutef, Qebehsenuef; sons of the son. Sons of the avenger.

The dark serpent in the night cavern is bound in chains. Each writhing movement causes the cuts in its body to open again, blood gushes out into the river of the Duat and with this the bones in the serpent's back glint in the light from the passing barque of the Flesh-of-Re.

And the winged uraeus, Semi, rises too. Fluttering feathered wings from the twists in its body, the cobra-head rises, tastes the air, turns - eyes darting towards the Barque of Re and the narrow passage that it must enter. Semi at last lifts the end of its own tail free of the sand, hangs poised in the air straight up, straight down, the image of the vertical, columnar; Semi, able to reach to the sky from the depths. In the small air currents, the form of Semi floats above the procession of the lord and the whirring of its wings will guide Re to the passageway.

Before the lord too is the boat of the Face-of-the-disk. The head is mounted, is transported through the Duat. Face-of-the-disk will appear as the sun - in darkness, in readiness for the stars.

Oh the stars to rise before the lord!

It is the star god, Unti, with the gods of the Unwearying Stars who tow the boat of the Face-of-the-disk, they tow through the night and the figure of Horus-Seth hovers near. Horus-Seth, mounted on uraei: two-headed, six-limbed, floating above the sand on bows - and the bows become curled about with the bodies of serpents writhing, writhing.

Oh you stars, what dreams do you carry before the lord? What essences, visions; what joys between all risings and settings - the movements of beauties, the warming moments of first solar rays on rocks and in crevices. Can the light of the stars penetrate to spaces between mineral particles, the cavities between micas and glasses in the grains of sand in the air? Starlight then reflected, refracted, dispersed; and the whirring of the serpent's wings, the flight of Horus-Seth, the passage of

Abesh, Fields, The-one-who-causes-to-breathe, and He-of-the-hour. Oh, the Face-of-the-disk in his boat before the lord; the hidden body, vast beneath the sand! Oh, Horus and the Sons of Horus: Hapy, Imsety, Duamutef, Qebehsenuef; the recollection in isolation of the vertical rise of all such gods! These vertical endeavours too - of Semi, the serpent in the air whose wings will beat, beat, beat!

For Seth has guarded the tenth hour of the Duat. Oh Seth: red god who brought about the death of Osiris! Seth, the force of storms and the ravaging destroyer; Seth, son of the sky goddess; Seth who tore himself violently at birth from the womb of Nut; Seth, the murderer, Seth, seeker after the fleeing Isis; Seth, pursuer of Isis' son, Horus; Seth - of combat; Seth, enemy of Horus; Seth - ravening god:

To protect the sun-god, Re!

Seth, come to the Barque of Re, give aid. Defeat darkness. Ride with the sun, defend the lord from the serpent of darkness. Seth, fearsome lord!

The figure of Horus-Seth floats nearer to the Barque of Re and near to figures struggling in water; figures drowning. Re calls out to them and to the goddesses who light the way to come.

And they respond. Hopefully, joyfully, with all the maidens, goddesses, those carrying the standard of Seth and they cry out:

Oh Re! You pass from the Tenth Hour of the Duat, Osiris' Underworld. Save the spirits. You enter the

192

ravine, you pass towards the eastern horizon accompanied by the Unwearying Stars. Re, in your barque, the dream throughout the darkness!

Re approaches the confined path, passes into it and emerges in the eleventh cavern of his journey through the Duat.

No lingering ba, unfit for Bakhu and the eastern horizon, may pass beyond this hour. And the solid darkness of the Duat, the thick night, dark night, the blackness of these ba-souls, will become the shadows, the gloom alone of the rising journey, the passage towards Bakhu and to a beginning of things. To depart from the dark which surrounds all: the coils of the serpent, the darkness of Apopis around the waters of Nun.

Oh Release! Refresh this blackness and the feathered shades will be removed. The first moment in indistinct, mottled light - and then no more. It is the angular projection of rock and masonry amid ripples on water which glimmers in the dark. The light of Flesh-of-Re is awaited - and the traces of eastern light within the cavern flicker.

Stars bear along the Barque of Re. Sobek-Re, and the Maidens of the Hours are seated on coiled serpents and each holds a star in her hands. They flicker, the light catches the most beautiful faces but the light is weak, and these images are far away - not restricted to the cavern, these stars float beyond reach: an infinite journey beyond the Duat. And the beautiful maidens whisper, glory in the faint light, and make careful gestures towards the lord of the light.

193

The Maidens of the Hours, the Bearers-of-stars, and the crocodile god, Sobek-Re are visions for the Unwearying Stars among the stars - and the Barque of Re is borne by them. Their cries will be sweet when the vessel becomes borne in the sky by Nut. And the four gods: bearers of light with bright discs held up, are able at this moment to reflect the light from the greatest traveller, from Re. The bright discs themselves are to shine like the sun. For all now await the very first moments: the first instant of warmth, the first moment of the shades disappearing.

The Distinguished-of-head in their white crowns of upper Egypt - and the bearded Mourners, the Wailers, and the Uniters in the red crowns of lower Egypt - and the bearded Nurturers and the twelve goddesses without names and all the other gods that bow down - and Mati, the cat-headed too - these move forward towards the train of Re, gesture their obeisance and adorn the noble travellers with their tall white crowns.

But these figures of the Duat weep for the lord of the Underworld, the dismembered king. For though their spirits rise up with their forms: massy, with silt from the Nile; with the growth of corn in the fields; with the hidden one; with the north wind on the river; with the wishes of all subjects for the pharaoh - these souls' forms would then be held to the earth - figures within the earth - and the star-forms would then become separated there. Thus would be heard the sounds of weeping; and gently at first the grief of all these figures would fill the cavern, pass through all of the gates - these sounds would then fill the dark space of the Duat entirely.

The lord Osiris - of grief. And the form of Isis flutters in the air, Isis descending upon the king - Isis: desire for the king.

The god set upright: the stable heart of the earth. Osiris, lord of the dead, and these helpers weep once the lord Re has gone. Cry for the departed light and the suffering of the lord Osiris! Hope in the procreation of Horus and the defeat of Seth! Can there be any act of justice these figures have not brought to pass; these indistinct forms, these weeping gods?

On their lord's behalf was Maat established by these figures next to the shrine of Re; by these gods was suffering ordained for figures seen in the Duat - and by their wish were others to pass time in the Field of Reeds. And yet their own fate would be to remain eternally: their stay in the Duat would be forever in darkness; they would remain in the night.

The body of Apopis is now chained to the ground. It writhes in death's agony, for here destruction of this darkness must become complete. Here no residue is to remain from the open wounds; no entrails spilled by the turning knives; no moments recalled when the eyes of the serpent might have burned a memory into the divine recollection - of Re; of the travellers with Re in the vessel; and of all in the Duat. For the victory to be complete, outer darkness must not in any way persevere.

The disturbances of the sand are to be removed - and the ripples on the water from the death throes themselves - these are to die away and all trace of blood in the water - and the serpent's cry, too, is to fade and die.

For, in the smallest crevices where no night creatures ever might pass, where the air is stilled for centuries, where no dust-motes dance, where no light ever penetrates, where no warmth is to be felt – nor even moisture - where there are no currents of air, no odours; no small vibrations, no cracking of rock surfaces, no fracturing of minerals: there in the dark, darkest moments which stretch unchanging backwards and forwards through unfathomable ages – there, the cry *could be* heard. It was the roar of the outer darkness: the blackness beyond the primordial waters, the coiling, turning malevolence kept at bay by the sun-god Re; the cry which is the death of the light.

On the prow of the Barque of Re a solar disc is mounted: Pestu the marvellous star is to guide the vessel along the paths in the eleventh hour, paths that fork and twist in the complete darkness. Here there is *Kekui Samui*: the darkness of the caverns of the Duat, the darkness of Apopis surrounding the swirling Nun. For by this star's aid the flickering light ahead will be attained and so shadow, *Keku Keskesu,* will enable the features of the vessel to be perceived from afar: no longer the illumination of the sun-god alone, but now also the light filtering from on high, through gaps and channels. There is to be a future beyond imagining for this journey, there will be victory complete for the lord of the sun, lord of the underground journey, lord of the day!

The great task of the serpent, Mehen, is now complete. Mehen, guardian of Re, who was able to twist, turn, defend, tear and gorge, who could envelop each foe, destroy the enemies of the sun; of light, heat, the new day; Mehen is caught up by Fa, by Ermenu, by Athpi, by

Netru, by Shepu, by Reta, by Amu, by Ama, by Shetu, by Sekhenu, by Semsem and by Mehni. The coils are carried on high by these gods: each undulation and silent breath rippling forward. The serpent uncoils from the canopy and from the figure of Flesh-of-Re - and the heavy, breathing form is carried above the heads of the gods, towards the faintest flicker of light ahead, to the rocky channels ahead, and to where rays stab outward, reflect on moisture on the walls; and where air currents drift downwards.

The odours of another world. The first trace. On the bank of the river are the goddesses Mistress-of-the-blessed-dead, Mistress-of-the-living, Fierce-of-horns, and Phallus-of-the-gods. On serpents' backs they ride, they move along the bank and travel first fast then slow; they move, always a little behind the Barque of Re - and their faces are shielded from this light: they never leave their serpent thrones. When Re speaks, they utter cries and acclaim him; at other times, they are silent and their spirits live upon the voices of the serpents which go forth from their feet daily. These goddesses live between earth and the Duat, their feet from which the serpents issue, are forever in complete darkness, the *Kekui Samui*, of the land of Osiris. Their arms and the upper parts of their bodies at times have been seen on the earth: in the desert landscape and around corners in dimly-lit alleys of cities at night.

In the Duat can be felt the first wind, with the first tastes of the dawn: the desert, the mists, and the seeds, pollens, the small fragments of aerial life. The winds rise sharply and come in gusts into the cavern. Sharp winds and against them the goddesses raise their hands.

197

Beautiful faces turned from the draught, hands raised before the faces, they ride their serpents and attend their lord.

Chapter Twenty-six

SPITTLE OF NEITH

Neith of Saïs and the festival of the lamps, the reconciliation of Horus and Seth, the goddesses with the Sons of Horus, death of Apopis.

Neith, the figure of the fecundator: of the red crown of the lower Nile; of the white crown of the upper Nile; the child.

Neith, Oh Neith, first mother, in the primordial waters. Self-begetter.

Neith, Oh self-generator Neith: to Re you are mother, wife and daughter. Glorious Neith! The sun-god, Re, passes in the Barque of Re; passes your four forms here. But these come forth on the echoing, come forth at the sound of Re; they are the guardians of Saïs, the unknown, the unseen, the invisible.

In Saïs, at the festival of lamps: and in the homes of those who might love you, the lights burn. On each table, in each alcove. On the first steps of each entranceway, joy, joy! The brightness in the night, the light in each corner. This celebration of your might.

Saïs, city of lights!

Principle of life - existing from the primordial chaos itself; all-pervading, self-generating, never to be suppressed. Oh First-to-give-birth, first mother, you are the self-creator - the maker of birth!

That you exist! Wife of Re, mother and child of Re: that which moves eternally and gives rise to all others, gives rise to the self!

> *Hail, great goddess within the Duat which is doubly hidden, thou unknown one!*
> *Hail, thou great divine one! Your garment has not been unloosed.*
> *Hail, hidden one! My entrance to you is not granted. Oh unloose your garment!*
> *Receive thou the ba of Osiris, protect it with thy two hands.*

Wise Neith from the primordial times, mistress of the bow, ruler of arrows. The children of Atum-Re, the Ennead themselves, call upon you! And Horus-Seth, the pacified, the aerial form of those who fought for the kingdom of the two lands in jealousy and in vengeance; Horus-Seth, six-limbed, now floats on your bow suspended in the air and dust of the Duat: reconciliation beyond all hope, reconciliation beyond imagining.

For the crime of dismemberment: the eighty years' struggle. And the children of Atum-Re have called to you, Neith, wise from the earliest times, creator of birth and the reconciliation of all:

> *To Horus the kingdom and to Seth: the gift of Astarte and Anat, daughters of Re.*

200

And Nephthys, Isis, Neith herself and Serquet - the goddesses who had shot forth flame in protection of the primordial waters - these goddesses protect also the dead viscera themselves:

I hide the hidden thing, and I make protection for Hapy who is in me, says Nephthys, lover of Seth. And the lungs are preserved.

I conquer the foe, says Isis, mother of Horus, *I make protection for Imsety who is in me.* And the liver is preserved.

Neith, reconciler of Horus and Seth, says: *I pass the morning and I pass the night of each day in making protection for Duamutef who is in me.* And the stomach is preserved.

And Serquet, the scorpion goddess, binder of Apopis says: *I employ each day in making protection for Qebehsenuef who is in me.* And the intestines are preserved.

Oh you Sons of Horus! See! See how you are saved!

But the child of Neith - of her spittle in the primordial waters cries out, the child is now dying.

He writhes, the son of darkness - Neith's own, in blood in the river of the Underworld, son of Neith who is mother of herself; child in agony: Apopis, the enemy of Re!

No more! Apopis, Apopis! Your mother, Neith, mother of all!

Apopis: the darkness! The deepest darkness in the Duat and that which surrounded Re in the waters of Nun. You are feared, serpent, for the terrible death after death: the final annihilation of all those whom you devoured.

All recollection gone, all remembered joys, all fears, and the darkness covers over each spirit in turn. There is no hope, there is no light, there will be no more sweet winds in the mornings at the fall of rain.

The dead husks, the forms without life; the recollection of stone pillars, dried residues at the bottoms of jars, the stains remaining on linen and windings for the dead. Only from these are the images of those you have devoured to be recalled. They do not live, they do not think or feel but as the wonderful light of the lord Re himself passes by your form, truth, truth is revealed and the spirits you have destroyed emerge. Your devoured ones, the victims of darkness itself appear a final time. Along your serpent's back the heads emerge. Each tormented spirit in that last agony as the flint jaws closed over him. The pain and terror preserved in eyes and the open, silent scream of your devouring.

Oh hatred, Oh Spittle of Neith! And the silent ones emerge: dried simulacra for the last time. The truth of Maat appears as the light of Re burns into your flesh! Your victims emerge a final time!

Oh Apopis, you have threatened and opposed the great god Re. In the Duat you have sought to engulf even Re himself, to plunge the sun-god into your eternal darkness. The divine head of Flesh-of-Re, sacred ram of the west, will never appear along the length of your serpent's back! Serquet has bound you. The Sons of Horus have held you in chains, your body is cut, it is bleeding and now Re will triumph at last. Over the blackness, the night, your outer darkness.

Isis has cut deep into the flesh, and Re, himself, will destroy the serpent of darkness.

Re, in your name of Mau - in your name of the cat - sever with hot knives each serpent's coil!

Each bone in the serpent's back becomes separated and the blood flows in the river of the Duat.

Aker, earth god who opened the gates at sunset to the changing sun-god, Oh Akeru, you many fearsome earth gods in the depths, imprison each severed coil!

Burn, stamp out and destroy each remaining piece, each evil fragment. Upon the dead remains of the fearsome blackness, men of the earth - of the two lands - stamp and tread, spit hourly upon the Spittle of Neith!
   Apopis of the night! Burn!

Chapter Twenty-seven

KHEPRI: THE SUNRISE

The goddesses of the pits, transformation within Life-of-the-gods, the forms of Horus, Khepri emerges, Nun personified raises up Khepri in the day barque.

The dawn. The dawn which follows is the first beautiful transformation. Light on the two lands and the wings of the Bennu bird, ba of Re, are to turn towards the sun. In the Duat, the last wickednesses are to be destroyed and the enemies of Re, followers of the darkness, who might escape the eleventh hour are trapped by the rearing head of Set-of-millions-of-years, guardian serpent - who will allow no evil-doers to leave, to pass from the Duat to the light and world above.

The goddesses of the pits will oversee the destruction of all such as these. In the first fiery chamber the spirits are seen through sulphurous fumes and in the fires they break open their own skulls and dash their brains on to the ground in pain. In the second fiery pit, the third, the fourth, the fifth each enemy of the greatest lord is burnt, is cut by the goddesses' knives. Such enemies are the Shadows, the Skulls and those who are cast down headlong: and Re addresses these forms and Set-of-millions-of-years will drive flames against them and the Lady-of-the-furnaces and the Lady-of- the-fiery-pits and the Lady-of-the-slaughtering-blocks and the Lady-of-swords will breathe fire on their bodies and their forms will be consumed completely. The second death. These enemies now: no more a threat to the rise of the great god, Re!

The dawn and such evil spent. All triumphs of the lord Flesh-of-Re achieved. The winds rise and the channel widens out. There will be transformations here for the trials of Re have been made complete. The labours, the spirits visited, their cries of joy at the light of Re - and the wailing cries as the lord of the sun moved on. Re must now move to the widest channel of all and through the twelfth portal, Reckoner-of-the-gods, and there meet the wonder and joy:

Wonder. The serpent, Life-of-the-gods. Transformation: all moments summed, all partial visions of pain and of endeavour completed. The fears and the night encounters that here will be wonderfully changed. The dark, feathered shades that flicker over the form of the dead god, sun-god, Flesh-of-Re. The companions in the Barque of Re - the guides and defenders - move the Barque of Re towards the tail, serpent's tail: in the opening from the Duat the fresh air blows across the dry sand where the glimmer from the upper lands penetrates.

The wonder and transformation in the body of the serpent itself. The work of He-who-is-upon-his-sand, Seker in the depths, unseen one of the underworld-of-the-Underworld will here be completed. The images of the scarab throughout the Duat: in the vessel, Isis-as-

Hathor; and upon the mount of sand, and in the stone balcony.

Every occurrence of the image of the rising lord Khepri, of the transformation towards life of the day - and the beetle rises with the sun, sphere of the sun. Khepri, The Becoming, the lord of the elevation of the sun!

And the serpent, Life-of-the-gods, gives rise to the first appearance, first form of the young sun; red rays stretching over the desert landscape from the eastern horizon - and from the Bennu bird in flight in the far distance with the flash of wings in the morning; eternal rebirth:

Oh we may therefore be glad! See! See!

The lord of the sun rises from all darkness, burns, tears, destroys all that was once feared. There is the light on gold wings and the sight in the far distance of the rise of Horus in the red rays stabbing outwards. Horus-of-the-horizon, Herakhiti. Our rising lord, Horus, in the air above the sands, circling, and in the Field of Reeds: his vision also. This god will bathe in the morning light: each drop of water will then sparkle, refract the light and coalesce; each drop falling from the divine wings, the origin of all colour and brightness itself. Glad! Herakhiti rises, flies in the air!

And Harmachis, Horus of the giant Sphinx: the shades move over the desert face. The shadows of eyes, chin, the beard; and the eyes stare into the red light itself for Horus is on the horizon, Horus rises: his image on earth is brightened each moment. The winged disc of Horus of

206

Behdet: the first arc on the distant horizon, the region of the gods, Field of Reeds; the red light bathes Herakhiti, and each particle is set in vibration, in sympathy with the vision of retribution, vision of the might. The image suspended - of the winged disc about to appear. Each moment to follow and the unworthy, the evil forms beneath will then be hunted down. A terrible pursuer, blocking off the sky: forming and re-forming, the brilliance of each ray and its origin; the stars dispelled in its light. All moments of eradication, elimination – Horus supported by the bright wings, downward draught - the fiercest winds arising at dawn. And the light from the sky contains this single vision and there is to be no respite on the earth. Over Egypt, over the Nile, in Nubia, Gubla, the seas to the north and south; in Punt. Oh, Horus of the winged disc! Avenger!

Khepri, you form and re-form. The beetle and the growth of its young. The sphere is to be seen, held in the beginning - of the day, of the world, of light - of all shadows dispelled from crevices; of all cool regions under rocks and by palace walls: the life of small insects, of lizards still in the night. These heartbeats, the breath in cavities, silence in the small places. Rocks crumble imperceptibly. Desert winds arising at dawn turn the air in recesses and silences retreat. The flight of insects and movement of reptiles warmed in the sun: all forms draw in breath; air passes down narrow passages to soft tissue within; carapaces expand and wings engorge. Hearts pump and the tissues rigidify: the first motions of creatures close to the ground. There are movements to precede flight: the small vibrations which might cause vortices to curl away, which give rise to directed draughts, which change the slightest of eddies into the largest circles of dust, of sand. The rays then pass among leaves and brick structures and onto undulations in the river-bed and beneath clear passages of water.

In the deepest part of the lake the image of the beautiful flower appears: deep, deep. As wings vibrate the petals open wider and the image enlarges, broken by the reflections on wavelets and ripples. It is intersected by floating reeds and by shadows. The flower then touches the water surface, rises from the water and blooms.

Nefertum of sweet perfume, Nefertum of Ptah and Sekhmet, the sweet odours for Re:

Hail Nefertum who comes forth from Memphis, I have seen no evil.

The blue lotus in the red rays of morning will open wide and the delight of sweet perfume will pass before Re, in the Barque of Re: the god of the sun, sun rising as Khepri; the image, perfection of Nefertum. And the sun-god will increase in the stilled pool and the blooms, grasses and the climbing plants, the palms will burn at the brilliance of the sun ascending. Not one blemish, not one slight alteration from the wishes of the sun-lord. Everything determined and the delight of Re. No disordered flows, no unknown winds. The primordial waters swirling in chaos - stilled for the lord. Outside, the unknown: Nun - and Maat, Maat, now present in the desires of this world, desires of the lord Re. These outer chaotic currents - and within, where the mind of the sun-god demands, determines, creates, moves and is aware, in the cavity itself: the kingdom of the two lands, this Nile, this world. Oh Maat! The order of the sun-god, order of the world: desires, the divine mind - separated from the Nun, Maat is in the bright and silent centre, in the heart, mind, eye of Re. A wonderful journey. Outwards from the very forces within. Re in joy, in the currents of joys and fears. And all balance, equalities, each identity between suffering and ecstasy is present in the awareness of Re, forms the substance of Re. All secrets, everything that is known partially to a few spirits within, everything that remains at the centre, is indistinguishable from the substance itself, everything that forms the god: matter indivisible and the undifferentiated glory itself.

All which trembles at the disturbance upon the approach of armies, which moves fitfully when children make appeals among themselves; all this is the substance, the material which creates.

And Maat has accompanied the dead figure, Flesh-of-Re, and has been present at the elevation and the destruction of spirit-forms. Maat in the Barque of Re was present when Apopis, the greatest disturbing influence - that which lies beyond all harmony, beyond the beauty of the mind of Re - when Apopis, this influence, threatened to overwhelm the creating principle. Principle of love and the joy of all dwellers within: the forms within, spirits in the land of the great king - ba-souls in the realm of the Judge of the Dead.

Osiris, lord and king of the dead!

Within the body of Life-of-the-gods, the transformation proceeds. The Barque of Re pulled forward toward the serpent's mouth; and the light of Re stabbing outwards through scales and fissures spreads forwards to illuminate the first reaches of the mountain at Bakhu. The light touches the mountain top, is reflected there to the sky and in this light Horus, Herakhiti, the flight of the Bennu bird, the rise of the winged disc and the rays of the sun-god themselves appear in the kingdom of the two lands. All this can be seen and the radiance now begins to emerge from inside the gaping mouth of Life-of-the-gods.

There will be glorious moments to follow. In the serpent's mouth the light is blinding, white. Within this illumination the movement of first one forelimb - curved, it flicks round the open mouth - and then another may be seen. They vibrate and the jointed legs and moving mouth-parts then appear within the serpent's gape. The brilliant shape within raises itself up: the rounded form in white is now visible through the serpent's flesh. The scarab crawls, crawls to the air, The Becoming of Khepri. Oh birth, birth!

Re, you were in the west declining. Re-in-your-name-of-Atum you sank to the western horizon: dead sun, dead form, Flesh-of-Re, the ram-headed lord in the Barque of Re. The greatest traveller in the Duat and now the form within the Life-of-the-gods. Life, new life. On the eastern horizon the serpent writhes one last time and the shimmering and radiant shape is made apparent. On the wing-cases, in the iridescence, the bright fluid hues flicker over the surfaces; colours interfere among themselves: the origin of the white light, origin of the dawn. Crimson rays reach out. In the upper air rays are turned, scattered and Khepri, the sun appears red, livid, living.

Nun, the formless - and a foundation is raised within Re-in-his-name-of-Khepri; within his divine heart. Nun - no firmness, no standing ground but the heart of Khepri is of wisdom itself. All structures within the divinity, all ideas and all intentions: the forms of the things to come, of the created things and the created lands - the two lands and the trees upon them and the crawling things between. The animals to tear at the fronds of trees, to scratch at barks. All were contained within Khepri's heart. In Nun only the unformed matter, the absent idea. But in the heart of Khepri are the desires, designs, the forms and movements themselves. The god of The Becoming, of the new life. Rise upon the firm ground! The Mound and the soil of the two lands stretches between sediments and the trickling rivulets of the waters of Hapi. The beetle raises its new life, ball of new life in warmth, in the sun's rays. And the order, regularity, law, rightness itself, Maat is the form within. In the heart, Khepri begins anew and the Mound rises, the water disperses, the two lands then become dried by the sun.

But wonderful lord of the morning, of bright light on the horizon, you make anew - and within the Life-of-the-gods this transformation has become whole! The sun, the sun emerges: Khepri, new form of the lord Atum-Re, Flesh-of-Re. Creator, Khepri - the dawn!

Khepri, you roll the brilliant orb before you. Khepri, in Mandjet now, the day barque of Re: the bright sun, white sun, the flames, rays, searing heat. Nothing may escape your brilliance. Wonderful, wonderful! The orb above the transformed Flesh-of-Re! And the day barque turns in the waters of Nun.

No more the flow of the river of the Duat, no more the deaths and the burning pits - the dismembered, the second deaths - spirits with Khepri in your barque: rejoice, rejoice! The dawn!

The vessel is lifted up. Nun will move the sun to the sky. Welcome, welcome to the lord in the firmament of the day. In the heavens - wonder and beauty - is the figure, just perceptible, of the sky goddess herself. Nut: every point in the sky, every point on the horizon, every star and the passage of the moon in the day; of the crescent passing in the night. Nut lives and her beauty is the brightness of stars. No clouds in the sky. Nut, your body arches over the kingdom of the two lands. Nut, from Bakhu to Manu, from the north to the south. Over the cataracts of the Nile, over the delta, your arms and your legs stretch far to the four corners: to the region of Hapy, to the regions of Imsety, Duamutef and Qebehsenuef. Over all heads, over all reaches, over the Duat, over the earth-brother, Geb. Nut, mother of Isis and Osiris, of Seth and Nephthys!

Geb, holder of the serpents of the Duat, reaches up to the sky.

Chapter Twenty-eight

SOTHIS: THE MORNING STAR

Nut gives birth to the sun, morning over Egypt, Isis appears as the morning star, Unas devours the gods, Osiris as Orion, Unas among the stars.

All terrors of the Underworld spent, all fears within the Duat gone. Darkness beneath. Does any danger, any anger, any loss remain? Will Nut caress; will she both swallow and give birth to the sun of bright day? Nut - the stars on your naked form; and the becoming sun-god, Khepri, rises. Nun elevates the day barque higher and higher! The vessel is raised from the Underworld of Geb to the skies of Nut. The figure of Osiris is there in the skies and Osiris is the darkness, the justice, the death and the paradise of all.

Beyond Nut the waters of chaos. Nun, you raise the day barque of Khepri to where Nut herself defeats all disorder. Restraint and the containment of all random movement, force; the fluxes in the heavenly waters above all Egypt and Nut protects, the goddess saves. Birth-giver, mother of Osiris. The daily passage of the sun along the sky's body: the brilliance along the naked form - and there at Manu the sun's disc is consumed at night. The passage through the night in the Duat will become a passage through Nut's form to this dawn. Birth of the sun. Nut who brought forth Osiris, Isis, Nephthys and Seth; Nut, who screamed at the lord Seth as he tore himself bloodily from the womb! Nut, it is your own son Seth who is heard - at his own birth - to rage, rage!

Seth! Look, Seth! Nut gives birth to the sun at Bakhu in the morning!

And morning stretches over the land of Egypt. Great joy at the rise of Re-in-his-name-of-Khepri in the skies. In the desert the first rays touch the top of the Great Pyramid itself. Small animals now move and the hours begin their passage with the drawing of water and the cackling of geese. Where, where the divine forms? The invisible made visible and the fears and dangers, the hopes now of each traveller in the desert. The Nile boats with sails hoisted move in the gusts and eddies of the morning winds. Forms invisible move, they divide and coalesce.

The unseen made visible: *Sothis!*

Sothis, Sirius: star in the sky to rise with the inundation. Sirius - bright with the sun and the floods already moving in the highlands. Sirius, bright spark on the horizon - and the waters will surge and the boats creak. Timbers will swell and the banks will overfill. The black silt in the water and the movement of reeds in dark water.

There are dreams in the dawn light. In the chambers where red rays move. The completion of severe ambitions: the fulfilment of wishes, the moments when truth itself is in abeyance, when horrors are not apparent, when the movement of giant invisible forms in the desert landscape is no longer evident, when the aspirations take their proper place and the ordering of the day and the night is completed, exposed.

The deep blue of the morning sky and the first rays of the sun's disk on the horizon. The star is seen bright and beautiful. It is Isis in the east - Isis who rises - the invisible giant form with the sun. Sothis, the brightest star on her crown is the harbinger, she rises with the instants and the hours to float above the land. All spirits are seen to take a part. And the world of the delta and the river, of the trees and animals, and the winds and the storms and the inundation itself: all these are repositories of the good and the evil, of that which animates, which may be loved or may be served. Each moment and each fragment of matter enlivened, aware: the presence and the beneficence, the threat conceived and known in familiar forms. Each agonised severance of limb by hippopotamus in shallow water; the growth of emmer wheat from the silt of the Nile. Each element known and knowing: to be assisted, to be made a moment in the life of all. These collected influences, these concerns and assistances, the threats and the fears: each meet and collect, they coincide and render each other stronger still. Each influence finds its fellows. There are fears and forces; joys in the desert. What wonderful imaginings! Each spirit of all hopefulness!

Each spirit of emptiness. The pharaoh, Unas, dweller in Orion moves from the eastern horizon to the west. In the skies he journeys and the gods tremble. They have seen the pharaoh appearing in power - as a god to live upon his father and feed upon his mother.

Unas you stand with your guiding serpents upon your brow - and there is one which seeks out spirits for burning. Unas: Bull-of-the-sky, conqueror at will, you live on the beings of the gods, you eat their entrails.

Unas, turn your back on Geb for you alone will decide the fates of the gods of old.

The dream: the pharaoh eats men and lives on the gods. There is Kehau, his messenger, and Khonsu. Kehau it is who captures the oldest gods with ropes and the serpent with raised head watches over them. Kehau binds them and Khonsu strangles them for the lord and for the lord he tears out their entrails. And Shezmu cuts them for the king and cooks them on his evening hearth-stones. The king eats their magic and gulps down their spirits.

Unas, the oldest gods and the frail goddesses are incense in your burner. You have broken the backbones and taken the hearts of the gods. You feed on the green crown and the red. You feed on the lungs of the Wise Ones.

The thighs of the Old Ones are boiling in your cauldron - and the feet of their women too.

Unas, the pharaoh, travels the daytime sky and the night, devouring everyone he meets.

———————

The stars which turn. In the paths in the blue sky of the morning the recollection of the Egyptian night. The sun will blaze in the sky. Each point, each moment living in perpetuity. Fears and hopes, the residues of dreams. Oh wonderful imaginings. Sothis rises - and behind - the brilliance of Khepri, the morning sun. The night begins to fade. All standing by the river, in the fields and abandoned on the seas to the north and east praise the rise of the lord, the conquest by the lord.

Each fragmentary life in the two lands. The great river, the pharaoh, the gods themselves present too in the skies - and the wife of the lord of the dead: Isis, great-of-magic, rises with the day. It is Sothis in the skies. Bright light of Sothis and the presence now in the morning above the two lands.

Light of Isis in the skies above Egypt.

In each hour that will follow: the rise of each star seen and unseen, the stars in position in the day, stars obscured by the day. The decans rising - each constellation to follow the sun - Khau, Sah, Septet. They are stars in their places, they travel the sky and make obeisance to their lord.

The decans never to shine in the same sky as Re: stars fading with the rise of Khepri. These stars are present in invisible ways: their passing attractions and pulses - a web of close approaches forever in motion, each partially or wholly the knowledge, love, fear and gentleness between men.

And Sothis attends Osiris-as-Orion in the sky. The lord of the dead, lord of dismemberment, Osiris of the Field of Reeds with the gods, partaker of the tree of life, he who lives on the bread of eternity and the beer of everlastingness:

Osiris, your hunger and thirst are appeased by the sons of Horus: by Hapy, Imsety, Duamutef, Qebehsenuef. Osiris, lord of Abydos: Orion in the sky - of the Field of Reeds, of the Judgement Hall of the Duat, of the Hall of the Double Maat!

Here, here above the skies, above Shu and Tefnut rising above Geb, the earth; and Hapi, the Nile; above all these: Orion, lord of all in the company of Re! Triumphant, the passage into day.

And the lives among the stars. The emerging from the Underworld from dangers and fears! Khepri-in-his-name-of-Re ascends in the sky, in the day barque itself. Above the earth the waters of Nun support Re in the sky. Oh glory of the bright light! Unseen now, stars turn and among the bright points the gods may live.

And the men who become gods: pharaohs in each passage between the stars. Power resides in the small gestures between the worlds, the dimly seen spaces where the gods arise. Power resides in the centre, the special region where light intersects - in the pyramid depths, in the city's heart, in each unknown place, in these formless essences: the power of the earth. Fathers of all fathers - of the ba-souls of Pe, of the ba-souls of Nekhen - amid vegetation and the drip of rain on fronds at night. Night, the light of stars becomes reflected in the droplets on leaves; in the crescents on the wave tops; on the wetted lips of jars. Eyes sparkle and reflect the light of moon and stars. Wind rises over a silent land.

Light from every corner - and the special regions in the passages between. In the dim light figures amass. In the desert: the forms silent and unseen. Beside each rock, between the grains in the sands, in each residual flower: the forms, gods, small crawling creatures, essences. The known forms, strange forms, images before the lord.

Unas among the stars. The gods tremble to be visible at last: in the passages in city streets, in the groves where distant figures move silently into caves, in depths.

Depths and the life springs upward and devours all around. Flesh for the pharaoh, the ravening god. Hunger: Unas pursues the deities among the stars. All powers to be controlled, joy to be possessed. The old, tired, the defeated gods:

Limbs might be fractured, bodies might be bent under heat and light among the stars. Pursued, strangled, boiled, burnt, torn asunder. For each the backbone to be cracked, for each the hungry tearing by Unas' teeth.

Unas triumphs over weaknesses. Unas, terrifier of the gods. In the journeys in the heavens, as the pharaohs rise, as the sun ascends and circles, as first one decan and then the following rise with the sun, as they mark the passage of the hours of the day - as each such constellation rises, therefore - in the midst of all such stars the weak and defeated are captured and devoured.

The pharaoh, possessed of power: to ascend through the many stages of power. The pharaoh to transcend death and the influences of others. This identity, this certainty: the desires and the hopes and the anger.

The dreams will grow in the heavens. About separated centres, about moving vortices, about bright stars themselves.

In the sea of beauty the sun-god will rise and each fluctuation and each eddy in such seas will appear brilliantly illuminated - these the centres of identity themselves. And Re will move in the waters in the sky held on high by Nun. In the light of Re, each separated refraction, current, twist and motion - the brilliants in the waters - will reflect between the sky and the seas; the gods in the day.

The heavens are to be sustained: each link and motion about a point. Min to appear and Osiris to be present in the heavens: Orion and Sothis and the journey through the skies invisible during the day. All pharaohs, stars, deities - the judge of the dead - to give deference to their lord: of light, of the inestimable power and the creation of all. Such vortices circle and spin away. They will be moved, carried with the sun in its journey.

In the two lands the deserts are peopled by the invisible gods. The forms arise from the rocks and scattered living remnants. In each element of shade the small, crawling life which once flickered over palace walls before Unas' eyes - which fell to the pharaoh's desire: *eat, eat!* - is always to be seen. And there are gods of the desert; of flowers, grasses, trees; of beetles and lizards; of each mite between sand grains - and gods of serpents approaching tombs. Each form which might wriggle, grow, live parasitically between fingers and toes; each form caught in the bright light of the day. And there are the gods too - of each form which welcomes the day, which scuttles towards the sun; of leaves which grow in the sun - and all figures and the tendrils of decay. All these spirits and forms possessing the divinity itself. And Unas possesses so very much. Unas devours the slaves and conquered heroes: the kings, soldiers, mothers, the women in childbirth, children of the day.

Chapter Twenty-nine

THE IMPERISHABLE STARS

Hor sees the stars from the Field of Reeds, the gods are safe among the Imperishable Stars, the world soul: the Ba.

The gods, the gods between the stars. The waters where writhing, frog-headed, snake-headed darknesses and nothingnesses move. Oh the infinities, their very selves! Curling, in swirls, these spaces between the stars. In terror through these formless wastes the specular presences of gods in defeat may fly.

Invisible now in the day, the brilliance of the day-time sun will obscure from view the dark presences and the feeble essence of each star.

On the sand the forms of unseen gods arise. The erect and demanding form of each deity may be perceived - and the maidens from the Duat might be seen in deserted streets in cities. These presences unknown.

All, all about, the lives, secrets, desires; each separated moment becomes recollected: the lives by the Nile.

And death in the river: Hor in the Field of Reeds gliding in bright light and hope. Such will be the essence and the joy of the life in the field of Osiris' kingdom. Hope rising; present in the minute reflections, each small contained point of light reflecting each other point - and the face of Hor, the reeds, the gliding flat boat. Oh the aspirations in each glimmer, each moment caught in no time. Each flicker on the face of Hor, each bright point in the sky and brilliant in the wavelets. Here the network is an unending series of reflections in each curved surface and on each fragment of shining metal; on water droplets, droplets within vapour, wettened surface of pebbles, the rain on leaves and in the boles of trees; reflections in tired eyes - and the world slips away.

In the rays of sun the image of hope will be multiplied in each reflection. Each moment to be summed, every view within the Field of Reeds a mosaic of bright lights - and hope will then enter the form of the spirit.

The mind of Hor, heart of Hor; of Hor the dreams, supplications, small movements, slight gestures - of Hor, mementoes of attractive motions of all persons upon first encounter. Hope then to become reflected in the eye; a millionfold in each drop.

Oh Hor in your boat you will never be restrained! The confines are only the wide expanse of the horizon. Broader than the skies, light from the skies - and the reeds will grow endlessly in the distant water.

Hor, connected with the lightest currents of the world. Hor with the sun's birth and the moments in memory when joy overflowed - when the first tear came, the first sigh was heard.

Forever with the slow lapping of the boat, with the palms which give dappled light, with the sway of reeds in light breezes, with the cool of the winds from the north - winds of Hapy; winds from the south - of Imsety; from the east - of Duamutef; and from the west - of

Qebehsenuef. Oh Sons of Horus rejoice, it is Hor in the Field of Reeds!

Hor can look up to the positions held by the stars when the sun is not with them: the form of Osiris in the heavens and the beauty of Sothis. The beauty of the night sky visible at dawn, the pursuit and the death of gods in the sky.

The terrible pursuits of Pharaoh Unas in the skies - and the minor, tired gods are then to die. Unas of power and the serpents rise.

Oh cries, cries of the death of gods. These resound in the skies and Unas' power overwhelms them. Stars of Nut's body devouring; the birth of the sun and the fading stars move: the beautiful form.

The firmament: the stars and the spaces between in darkness. In these terrible places the refuges. Oh beautiful mother, Nut over the two lands and the four corners: the tresses of the Sons of Horus will support these heavens.

In the north, the Imperishable Stars turn. Each path will circle the pole and the Unwearying Stars which rise and set, which have accompanied Re on his journey through the Duat; these stars carry with them through the skies, along the body of Nut, the new light of the sun; Re of the bright light casting shadows. The heat of the day.

These Unwearying Stars, where Unas roams, descend to the journey underground. They are the decans that mark the passage of time; the stars where Osiris dwells; these invisible stars where the beauty of Sothis reigns:

Pull, pull the barque of the day, the god Re is risen and the light penetrates all!

These territories among the stars. The tracts, the darknesses and blinding light. At each point the forces meet, swirl about each other and the pursuit proceeds. In centuries these outcomes. And the Imperishable Stars shine: the bull, Meskheti, circles and the back of the hippopotamus, Reret, is mounted by the crocodile. She is the mother beast of the skies and there is Horus-the-warrior: Horus-as-An. The battle has raged amid these forms with Serquet in the sky. In these revolutions, the sanctuary, the glory.

The beautiful ascent of the pharaohs to the stars, to the crystal floor of the skies. These Unwearying Stars revolve. These angers, joys and deaths into the night: in the silence between the stars and in the turning movements beneath the earth.

The refuge: the permanent, the circumpolar stars. These stars untainted forever in the sky. The Imperishable Stars never to descend to the earth and to the Duat: polar stars in the north, the circling dance. Oh may perfect essences be the companions of the pole!

Spirit-forms. In every corner, in every dust-filled cavity; in the Delta and in Nubia, Libya and Punt; in the four seas and in the cold regions, across far seas; in the shadow of the pylons at Waset; in the spaces between reeds in the river; over the glistening tops of pyramids and in the small spaces in street corners; in birth chambers and in the footsteps of Min; in the cracks in tombs through which lizards and snakes might crawl; in the shadow from rocks newly fractured by the heat - in the desert peopled in the invisible way - in hidden places the forms coalesce.

The Maidens of the Hours. In the far distance; on the distant horizon; in every hot wind that blows into temple precincts; in every glimmer in the eye, in the Eye of Re; in the oceans churning in the east; in the tombs of the west; in the dark moments between the flickering of flames and the glinting of metal; in each moment of pain from the severed limb, the fracture; (and the burnt and dying, the drowned corpse gives forth the dead breath, dead cry) - in each such recollection there is the rattle of empty final moments, the summed moments of joy and despair.

Oh these hours! Centuries pass in the dry air. There is the flicker of sunlight, the reflection on burnished leaves. Hor's hope: outcomes seen through the corner of the eye, the time when flickering light on low bushes dispels concentration - and fears that have accumulated over the years. Such fears are brought to mind by light between moving fronds, cavities among leaves in eddies in vapour. Sunlight rises from the leaves' upper surfaces and the eye in contemplation picks out delicate features. Hope, each beautiful curl.

The spirit flies, the spirit increasing. There are distances spanned and blooms in the desert are shaded from the sun.

On the dry earth a moment of contemplation and the ba-souls and the moving forms approach: the minute insects on the walls where the pharaoh might sleep; writhing snakes that might enter the necropolis, enter the tombs, unite with the flesh, the khat of the son of Ankhori and Karem drowned in the Nile. Hor, priest of Montu and opener of the gates of heaven at Waset. The snakes become the form of Hor, of the dweller in the Field of Reeds and the world is to become suffused in bright hope. The figure in the desert wet with rain emerges: the ba of Min, the akh of Min; the heart, shadow, power of Min - and the desert is alive, inhabited in this way, invisibly the ba-souls move and are pursued, the remnants of the living, gloriously living. Serpents, serpents, the khat of Hor.

Among the stars the akh-souls are transformed. Each a coalescence of light, the feeling, seeing heart of awareness suspended in currents among the stars.

Such joys of permanence and each small being might join - as the serpents might drift - in warm, supportive currents in passages between the stars. Below are the terrors of life and death and of the Duat. The fires, lakes of fire, the echoes and the silence of falling dust on exposed surfaces; the cries of the enemies of Re and the scream, too, of the lord in despair: last cry, death of Osiris.

The despair becomes - as the great Flesh-of-Re becomes Khepri in the morning - this despairing cry becomes the hawk-headed and unseen form of Seker, lord on his sand. Living, the moments emerge, they are divine, divine life of the nights and years. Each decan rises, marks off days and nights in small divisions: each flood of the Nile, each ripple of the cataracts and the swirling of winds in the desert. Winds at dawn and the scorpion, Serquet, scratches and is found under the sand. The serpents slide beneath temple steps. Shade in the heat of day. The two lands united: each separated moment, each death in the river. The moments when the sun rises over pylons and obelisks, over pyramids. The light settles over distant earth works.

The moving forms are visible particularly. They gave rise to the pharaoh's night tremors. Fears over the acquisition of power: the growing awareness of the groves and forests, of ages past.

Ba-souls of Pe and ba-souls of Nekhen who guard the pharaohs: oh this darkness between the trees!

What is seen, what may be seen - from the glance, the fearful stare - the sudden exposure of a limb or a lock of hair?

All dreams of fears: the cries of the suffering imagined - and the images of gods, of attributes, powers and loves. Oh these desires! The fragments are made and the dreams have lasted for the centuries, the thousands of years. Each continued form, each staring eye and twisted limb: the mothers, children in dreams, the entwining tresses - and branches of rich green growth.

Small sounds are to be heard; the pursuits among distant waterways and in corridors within the city. Oh the lights carried through passages and into chambers. Lights that shine in alcoves which glisten, glisten. There are remembered fragrances. Blooms on rigid stems dying. There are great endeavours accomplished and waters flowing; flights through passages, every moment floating above marble floors: moments suspended above pedestals on entering small enclosed spaces. All to become aware fearfully, aware that behind this pillar, behind this tapestry - the deity, the power, the presence in the dark of the origins and the ends. The dream of the passage of the day barque through the stars: within these waters the spirits survive, spirits with the whirlpools of great influences about them.

The dream of Egypt itself. In the northern skies the Imperishable Stars turn and there in joy live the gods free from fear. Their silent communication - and the pharaohs, entered upon the divine, in the starry skies. From the green origin of things each ba of Pe and ba of Nekhen resides there in glory: Unas, pharaoh, never to be there.

The stars, the stars with glory between. Hor, in joy, is able to see the light pass among them. The whole body itself, this world with the men and women in it, the lands and the foreign mountains, deserts, seas, each rock and known place so represented, and each creature living there; all the earth and the stars above it - the *Body* itself. The mummiform khat of Hor and the serpents within. This *Body*, of Osiris, of Neith: the heart of the earth. Each flower the outgrowing and Hor the outgrowth too.

And the *Ba,* soul of Osiris is the soul of Re, of Neith and of Geb - is the *Soul* of this world, wide universe untold. The goodness and the light swirl, turn about each other, forms arising, joining, involuting. The *Soul* of all that is, of gods and the world evolving, of the sun of the Underworld of Egypt, of the son of Ankhori and son of Karem. Of Hor, of skies above.

———————

Other Books by Peter Preston:

"Corridor Dance"   *"Vertical Line"*